JOINT VENTURE

JOINT VENTURE

CAROL RHEES

Joint Venture

ISBN: 979-8-9865206-0-5

Cover design: Lynn Andreozzi
Interior design: Jennifer Toomey

Dedicated to

my incredible muse Claire and

my husband John who was at my side every

step of this unexpected journey

POPLAR POINT

October 1969

Alice pumped her legs furiously, her swing arcing ever higher, finally reaching that point in the sky when there was suddenly, for a second in time, slack in the chain.

"See if you can touch the branch with your feet, Helen," Alice called to the girl swinging next to her, their rhythms matching perfectly.

"I did it!"

"Me, too!"

The girls' shrieks of delight echoed across the playground.

Alice was thrilled to have found a new friend. Holding tight to the swing's chains, she hazarded a quick look at Helen, taking in her neatly–pressed red plaid dress, knee socks, and whitened saddle shoes. Awfully fancy for a day at the park, she thought. A twinge of uncertainty passed through Alice as she looked down at her own slightly too short jeans, flannel shirt, and scuffed shoes of unknown origin. Oh, well. "Let's do it again!" she cried. The girls resumed their enthusiastic pumping,

"Helen!"

Startled, both girls reluctantly dragged their feet in the dirt, slowing their swings and turning to see the source of the interruption.

Helen's mother, Margaret, was rapidly approaching.

"Get over here right now! I told you never to play with that girl."

"But, Mommy, we were just swinging."

"Helen, do as I say."

Alice looked at Helen, who gave her a sheepish shrug of the shoulders. "Bye."

"Bye." Alice watched Helen reluctantly grasp her mother's hand and follow her out of the playground. They hurried across the town square with its towering maples, now flaunting their brilliant fall colors.

PART I

Poplar Point
Fifty Years Later

CHAPTER 1

ALICE

Alice's tires squealed embarrassingly as she accelerated her old Subaru out of the church parking lot and around the corner onto Main Street. She wasn't usually a fast driver, but tonight's meditation session had been exasperatingly difficult. Now, she was anxious to get home, settle herself in her comfortable old rocker, and relax after a hit or two from a well–rolled joint.

As Alice was rounding the curve at Sharky's Bar and Grill, she suddenly hit the brakes. A pastel figure in heels had just stumbled from the bar's front step and fallen flat on the sidewalk no more than twenty feet away.

Alice hurriedly pulled the car to the side of the road, put it in Park, and climbed out. She cautiously approached the pink and green mound moaning softly on the sidewalk. She looked closely at the prone figure and noted the carefully highlighted and coiffed hair glinting in the soft light of the streetlamp. *Good God, it was Helen Newbold!* Alice hadn't seen a lot of Helen since she and Mr. Perfect Jack Roberts had high–tailed it out of town right after graduation. But Poplar Point was a small place, and Helen had been around enough visiting her mother and daughter that Alice recognized her instantly—even face–down in the middle of the sidewalk. Alice bent over and shook Helen gently, calling her name.

Helen lifted her head and peered at Alice with bleary eyes. "Oh, no. Is that you, Alice?"

"Yes, Helen." Alice did her best to sound sympathetic. *Crap, this was awkward.* Alice would have preferred to walk away, but she couldn't leave Helen like this. She had obviously been drinking heavily, the perfume of her most recent martini sitting heavily in the air.

As Alice helped Helen to her feet, she felt a small vindictive flare of pleasure. She tried to suppress it, remembering the silent commitment to kindness and compassion she had made at the meditation meeting just moments earlier. Well, this was definitely a test of her commitment.

Despite having grown up in the same small town and having known each other for years, she and Helen had never been friends. Indeed, by high school, they had actively disliked each other. Helen, Homecoming Queen and head cheerleader, had exhibited nothing but disdain for Alice and her not–cool friends. Memories of Helen's scornful and condescending treatment of her still stung even after all these years. And then there was that weird thing between their mothers—some deeply felt grudge match that went back years but was never spoken of or explained.

Helen appeared to be recovering and was clumsily straightening her clothes as she pulled herself into a sitting position.

"Don't worry, Helen. Are you staying at Kim's? I can take you to her house," Alice said in her most reassuring voice.

Helen looked up with a panicked expression. "Oh no, please! I can't let Kim see me like this. Maybe we could sit in your car for a few minutes?"

Alice thought of Helen's daughter Kim, the local high school principal and chair of the town's Board of Selectmen. Kim was a lovely young woman, but Alice could certainly understand that Helen might not be comfortable showing up at her house in her present condition.

"Of course. Here, let me help you up." Alice led Helen by the elbow to the car. Before she had even gotten the door closed, Helen burst into tears. *Wow! Helen must have tipped back more than a few.*

Alice walked hurriedly to the driver's side and got in. "Helen, what's wrong?" she asked, turning in her seat. *God, Helen did look awful.*

Helen paused to take a breath. "I'm having a tough time."

No shit, Sherlock. Alice faced back forward and put the car in gear.

"I'll tell you what. Let's go to my house. You can call Kim and tell her you'll be a little late getting back, then clean yourself up and have a cup of coffee. I can get Bear to bring you back here to get your car. How does that sound?"

Helen sniffled, then nodded.

CHAPTER 2

HELEN

Helen tentatively trailed Alice across her front screen porch with its dream catchers and faded Buddhist prayer flags. She tried to take it all in. *What a strange porch.*

"Come on in, Helen. Why don't you call Kim while I go make us some nice strong coffee?"

Helen nodded, instantly regretting the sudden movement of her head.

As Alice headed into the kitchen, Helen looked around the living room critically. A mishmash of old, worn furniture filled the room—probably the same furniture that had been there when Alice was a girl. Nothing matched. There wasn't even a discernable color scheme. And it had the strangest smell. Still, she had to admit—the room did look comfortable, in a thrift shop kind of way.

Helen reluctantly fished in her purse for her phone. What in the world was she going to say to Kim? *Hi Kimberly, this is your mother. I got drunk and now I'm at Alice's?* Kim would think she had lost her mind. *Kimberly, this is your mother. I've had a slight attack of appendicitis and gone to the hospital. I'll be home later.* No, that's totally unbelievable. She obviously had to lie, but it had to be at least somewhat plausible. What could she say she was doing in this dull, claustrophobic little town where she didn't have a single friend?

Helen's hands shook slightly as she looked at her phone. *Buck up, girl. This is just your daughter you are calling.* But then again—it was

Kimberly with her thinly veiled looks of disapproval, carefully tailored and pressed navy–blue suits, and rigid ideas of right and wrong. Helen was no marshmallow, but somehow she had produced a daughter who was more than her match.

"Kimberly," Helen whispered into the phone.

"Mom? Is that you? Do you have any idea what time it is? Where are you? Are you hurt?"

"No, no—I'm fine. I ran into a few friends in town and I'm at one of their houses. Just reminiscing about old times. I didn't want you to worry."

"That's ridiculous. I didn't even know you had any friends here, and it's already 10:30. You need to come home."

Helen bristled. "I'll be home soon. You don't need to wait up or anything."

"Of course I won't wait up! I have to be at school at seven tomorrow, and Kevin and the kids have to be up early, too. Please be quiet when you come in. Really, Mom."

Tears began to swim in Helen's eyes again as she put down the phone. What an awful night. What had she possibly been thinking walking into that old dump, Sharky's? She had wanted, no needed, a stiff drink, and drinking at Kim's house under her watchful and disapproving eye had not been an appealing option.

Helen watched Alice walk in slowly from the kitchen, balancing two old china cups on saucers, mismatched of course. She couldn't resist a closer examination of Alice, whom she had not spent any real time with in years. Yup, not much had changed except for the 20 or 30 extra pounds. Same hippie–dippy clothes. Same dangling earrings and jangling bracelets. Same long thick braid down her back—only now it was gray instead of brown. Unconsciously, Helen brushed her palm over her own recently colored hair. Helen glanced at the many rings on Alice's fingers and noted that she still wore her wedding ring, despite the fact that her husband Arlo had died at least a year ago.

Alice carefully placed a cup and saucer on the table next to Helen's chair and settled herself in the old rocker. "OK, Helen, what's going on?"

Helen paused. Could she really be about to bare her soul to Alice of all people? But the words, unbidden, came out in a torrent. "Jack left me.

For our stupid administrative assistant, Brittany. She's half his age and has already had more plastic surgery than I have." The spigot reopened and tears coursed down Helen's face. "My lawyer called a little while ago. Jack's lawyer is sending divorce papers." Helen's lower lip quivered as she absorbed the look of surprise on Alice's face.

Alice shook her head slowly. "Sounds like your typical mid–life crisis to me."

Helen stared blankly at Alice.

"You know. Men reach a certain age, feel vulnerable, start questioning their virility—and bingo, a newer model is in the picture. A romp in the hay and the man feels like his old self."

"Maybe." Helen felt terribly uncomfortable. She cautiously tested the coffee.

"Sounds like you're better off without him while he sorts himself out, Helen. What's happening to your real estate business in Boston anyway? I thought you and Jack were raking it in."

"We were. And don't you worry. I know the nastiest divorce lawyer in Boston. Jack will be paying me for years! But I can't possibly stay in Boston now. I'm sure you don't understand, but it's so ... humiliating. Brittany and Jack are everywhere! I can't bear to see them or any of our old friends at the club, and I certainly don't want to work with them. I don't know what to do." Helen took a deep, shuddering breath. "I thought I could come back here and figure everything out. But now I remember how much I hate it here. This place is the pits. It's like the town got caught in a time warp or something." Helen shivered. "There's no one here I can be friends with, and Kim and Kevin have their own lives.

"I never thought I'd be envious of you. But you're so plugged in here, so comfortable," Helen continued as she looked at Alice plaintively. "You've never even tried to be attractive and you still have so many friends." A tear ran down Helen's cheek.

CHAPTER 3

HELEN

CRACK! THE SOUND OF THE porch door slapping shut startled both women. Alice's son, Bear, strode into the room, trailed by his tired old German shepherd, Toby, and the sweet hint of a recently smoked joint. Helen recoiled slightly, taking in Bear's thick beard, "Weed the People" tee–shirt, and dirty jeans.

"Ma, have you seen the paper? Do you believe this? It's all everyone is talking about. I think this could be the salvation of Poplar Point! All it needs is someone with some business know–how and some cash to get started!"

Helen, wiping the streams of mascara off her face, surreptitiously took in the headline of the paper in Bear's hand: "Town Meeting to Vote on Marijuana Sales; Town Leaders in Uproar." A picture of an angry clergyman, clenched fist raised high, accompanied the article.

"Well, I don't know," said Alice, her hazel eyes scrunching thoughtfully. "There was a lot of heated discussion before tonight's meditation. Poor Timmy could never get everybody focused. This could be a tricky business."

"It shouldn't be too tricky. Growing marijuana is cheap, and the demand is huge! In Colorado and other states, people are making millions!!"

Helen's head suddenly cleared. "Millions?" she asked in a low whisper.

Bear turned to look at Helen. He smiled.

"I'm sorry. Didn't mean to ignore you. That was awfully rude of me. Aren't you Helen Newbold, Kim's mom? I remember you from when Kim and I were in high school. We used to hang out during the summer while Kim was staying here with her grandmother. Are you back in town now?"

"For a while," Helen whispered, a spasm of pain flitting across her face. Helen caught herself. She was not going to cry in front of this scruffy man who looked like he would benefit greatly from a bath and a decent haircut. Helen pulled herself up. "Do you actually think a marijuana business could take off here?"

"Hell yes. The suppliers and demand are already in place, and my dad's old store would be a perfect location. And we've got the money from my dad's life insurance. Ma and I just need someone with the business know–how."

Helen noticed Alice's eyes flash with irritation. "What are you talking about, Bear? *We* don't have any insurance; it's my insurance and my financial security. For that matter, it's my building, too."

Uh oh. Helen glanced worriedly from Alice to Bear. Bear looked like a little boy who had been scolded in front of the class. A mix of embarrassment and annoyance played across his features.

"I'm sorry, Bear. That was a little harsh. It's definitely something worth investigating, but later. Helen has had a rough night, and I'm sure she's not interested in hearing about our family matters."

Helen remained focused, though, on the possibilities of a new money–making angle. She knew absolutely nothing about marijuana, but she desperately needed a business idea—a way to prove to herself and to Jack that she could stand on her own. She stared hard at Bear. "Bear, that's an interesting idea. What's the deal with the Town Meeting?"

"Well, you probably heard the state legislature legalized recreational marijuana. But they left it up to each individual township to decide whether to allow the commercial sale of marijuana there. The Board of Selectmen in Poplar Point has already announced its opposition to a store here. But I think there's a lot of people in town who think a store's a good idea, and it's ultimately up to the town, not the Selectmen, to decide."

"Bear," Alice said, attempting to change the subject quickly, "what are you doing here anyway?"

"Just dropped by to see how you're doin', Ma. Any dinner left over?"

"On the stove."

As Bear cruised into the kitchen, Helen stood shakily. "I think I better get going, Alice. Thank you for listening and being so kind."

"No problem, Helen. Can I have Bear drive you to your car, or at least walk you to Kim's?"

"Oh, no," Helen said hastily. "It's only a couple of blocks, and I can make it fine. I'll pick my car up in the morning."

Helen set out into the night. Stepping out of the fenced yard onto the uneven sidewalk barely lit by the flickering streetlights, she began rummaging in her bag. She must have some tissues somewhere! With a sigh, Helen's shaky fingers wound around a mound of crumpled Kleenex. She absentmindedly rubbed her cheeks as she worked her way back toward Kim's. This was so awkward. She couldn't believe she had confided in Alice of all people. She'd probably enjoy telling all her friends.

Helen walked on, her thoughts churning. A marijuana business! God, she sure would love to hit it big and leave Jack wondering what the hell he was doing with Brittany.

CHAPTER 4

ALICE

Alice woke the next morning as the sun rose. She knew she should get up, but many days she found it hard to get out of bed. Really, why bother? She didn't have a job to go to, a family to care for, a husband to look after. She was definitely stuck in the doldrums, as Arlo used to say.

With a sigh, Alice forced herself to sit up. After swinging her legs over the side of the bed and putting her feet on the floor, she repeated her morning mantra borrowed from the Dalai Lama:

I am fortunate to be alive. I have a precious human life, and I will not waste it. I am going to have kind thoughts toward others. I will not get angry or think badly about others.

There! Alice felt better already. Ever since Arlo died, she had worked hard to find a spiritual path that would bring meaning back to her life and set her on a strong path. With encouragement from Timmy Wentworth, director of the Live Strong Senior Center and erstwhile meditation leader, and his wife Willow, she had thrown herself into meditation and yoga, practiced mindfulness, read Thich Nhat Hanh and listened to the Dalai Lama. Alice got out of bed, pulled on her robe and slippers, and did a few unenthusiastic stretches to get herself moving. As she pulled up the shades, the sun poured in, and her mood lightened further. She took in the blue sky, fluffy clouds, and trees still heavily laden with leaves. Today was definitely a day to practice mindfulness!

As she brushed her teeth, Alice watched a shockingly red cardinal dart back and forth from the bird feeder outside her bathroom window. She stopped and listened closely. Yes, she could hear the soft splash of the surf as waves ceaselessly washed the sand along the nearby bay shore. She put the cap on the toothpaste and walked downstairs into the kitchen.

Alice fixed herself a cup of tea and settled at the kitchen table, preparing herself for a short meditation. But try as she might, her thoughts were jumping all around, repeatedly returning to the events of the night before. She tried to focus on her breathing, to observe her thoughts, and then let them float away. But mindfulness eluded her. Her mind was racing.

Alice had lain in bed for hours thinking before finally falling asleep. She knew Bear had been bouncing from one crappy job to another ever since Arlo's sudden death. Alice had asked Bear at the time if he wanted to take over his dad's liquor store, but Bear had been too devastated and had said no. Alice had understood. The magic was gone, and the thought of stepping into Arlo's shoes every day hadn't appealed to either of them. She hated that she had so off–handedly rejected Bear's ideas about a marijuana store, particularly in front of Helen. Bear probably knew every pot farmer, dealer, and user in the area. And he was right—Alice did have an empty store and some start–up capital. She had to talk to Bear and apologize again. But Alice was quite sure Bear had noticed how Helen had perked up at the mention of a marijuana business, and she had to make him understand that involving Helen was not a good idea. He knew she and Helen were not friends and that their families had always been estranged. Plus, all you had to do was look at them to know they were polar opposites!

Alice gave up on meditating and ate a quick bowl of granola and blueberries. She stood at the sink and enjoyed the soothing, silken sensation of the water running between her fingers as she washed her bowl. Just as she finished cleaning up, she heard Bear's truck turn into the driveway, its tires kicking up a rat–a–tat–tat of loose stones. Bear walked in, his imposing frame filling the doorway. Toby scooted in after him right before the screen slammed, a look of unadulterated hopefulness on his face.

"Anything to eat?" asked Bear. He gave his mom a quick hug and then, after eyeing the coffeepot, opened the refrigerator door and grabbed the milk. Alice watched him appraisingly as he sat at the table happily tucking into a large bowl of Cheerios, a few stray O's taking up residence in his thick beard.

Alice reached across the table to pat Bear's arm. "I'm sorry about last night, honey."

Bear glanced up, spoon paused in mid–flight to his mouth. "Sorry about what, Ma?"

Alice was quite sure Bear knew what she was talking about. "You know, my popping off about the store and the insurance. I wasn't comfortable, what with Helen here and all. I really do want to hear what you're thinking."

Alice was surprised when Bear responded immediately, laying out his initial thoughts on how to make a go of a cannabis business in Poplar Point. He clearly had put some thought into the matter. "I know it's totally up to you what you do with dad's store, Ma, but it does seem like the perfect place. It's a good–sized building in a good location with plenty of parking."

Alice nodded thoughtfully, taking a sip of her second cup of tea. In some ways, the idea of a marijuana store appealed to her, too. She certainly knew her way around cannabis, and she kind of liked the image of Arlo's old liquor store transforming itself into a pot shop.

"I was surprised to see Helen Newbold here last night, Ma." Alice looked up. Bear was studying her, curious to see her reaction.

"Yeah, me too." In fact, Alice still couldn't get over finding Helen sprawled on the sidewalk outside Sharky's. And then what a shock that Miss Goody Two Shoes had brightened up at the mention of a cannabis business of all things. In high school, Helen had been one of the "Just Say No" aficionados.

"Well, I got to thinkin' last night, Ma. Neither of us has the business experience we'd need. But everyone in town knows Helen and her husband have a super successful real estate firm in Boston. I don't know what's goin' on with her, but I got the sense last night she may be a bit at loose ends. I was wondering if she'd be interested in talking to us, maybe helping us—that is, if we decide to go forward."

Oh, no. Just as I feared. "I'd have to think about that, Bear. To put it mildly, Helen and I aren't exactly friends, you know. I have to tell you, I can't see us working together."

"I know, but think about it, Ma. This is an enormous opportunity for someone, and it might as well be us." Bear pushed back from the table, gave Alice a quick hug and headed for the door, Toby trailing behind him.

Alice watched Bear climb into his old truck and back out of the driveway. Damn. Maybe this was Bear's big break. He certainly deserved one, and she didn't want to be the one to stand in the way. But Helen? There was too much history, too many negative feelings. Best to leave that pot unstirred.

CHAPTER 5

ALICE

AFTER FINISHING CLEANING UP AND haphazardly throwing on some clothes, Alice climbed in the old Subaru and headed toward town. Before she knew it, she found herself turning into the parking lot of the weathered but capacious building that had belonged to her husband and now belonged to her. She pulled into a space at the edge of the lot and, after twirling the wedding band on her finger for a few seconds, got out of the car. Hands on hips, she stared at the building, remembering.

Alice and Arlo had not been married long when Arlo unexpectedly inherited the building from a wayward uncle. It was a huge break for them. For a time, she and Arlo had run an art gallery aimed at the summer tourists, featuring sandy landscapes and endless portraits of boats. But then Bear came along, and Arlo had decided a liquor store would be more lucrative. And indeed, it was. Alice and, later, Bear had loved helping out in the store until ...

"Alice! Is that you?"

Squinting, Alice could just make out Suzanne stepping out the front door of the store, a large box of old clothes clutched precariously in her hands. Alice forced herself to walk forward. "Here, Suzanne, let me help you with that."

Then, in a rush, everything came back, literally knocking the air out of Alice's lungs. Arlo crashing to the floor behind the cash register, his heart attack massive. Alice frantically calling 911 and then cradling

Arlo's head in her lap, begging him to stay. But he was gone before the ambulance arrived.

Suzanne, seeing Alice's face turn chalky white, dropped the box and rushed to Alice's side. "Alice, are you OK? Are you feeling faint? Here, bend over for a minute and put your head down." Suzanne cradled Alice in her arms, momentarily bearing Alice's full weight.

"I'm OK," said Alice after a moment, straightening and brushing a tear away. "It's just that, well, I haven't been back since…."

"I know." Suzanne kept a comforting arm around Alice's shoulder. "What brings you here today?"

"I had to see it." Suzanne gave her a quizzical look. "Bear is talking about opening a marijuana store here, and I had to see if I was ready."

"I know a lot of towns and businesses are talking about this all around the state. But, Alice, you need to remember that this is your building to do with as you please. Don't get pressured into anything."

"I know. But I don't want to stand in Bear's way if this is the right thing to do. It might even be good for me to see the store busy again with Bear running things. It's been a year, after all."

Suddenly embarrassed, Alice turned back to Suzanne. "I'm sorry, Suzanne. I'm being so selfish, ignoring how all this affects you and your thrift market business. I know this has been a good place for you to store and sort everything, and it has been wonderful knowing you've been here."

"Don't be silly, Alice. Our lease is up in a month, and there are plenty of spaces around town I can use. I never envisioned this as a long–term arrangement. I'm more concerned that you make the right decision for yourself."

Alice squeezed Suzanne's hand. "Well, who knows what will happen? Just keep this under your hat for now, if you don't mind, and I promise I'll keep you posted."

CHAPTER 6

HELEN

HELEN STARED BLANKLY OUT THE window. It was a glorious morning, but the blue sky and warm breeze barely registered. Her head was pounding so badly that even her teeth hurt. Just thinking about last night made her feel like throwing up. What had she been thinking? Helen wasn't averse to tipping back a few drinks, but she couldn't remember ever having tied one on by herself in a bar full of strangers. And what had Alice thought? If Alice had recognized her, had other people, too? Perhaps it was time for a little makeover. She was tired anyway of the same old muted preppy look that had worked in Boston but stood out like a sore thumb in Poplar Point. Helen's eyeballs ached as she scrolled through the screen on her phone looking for a nearby hair salon. Maybe blond? Red?

The shrill ring of Helen's cell phone made her cry out in pain. She looked at the caller ID. Jack? Helen hesitated, then answered in as confident a voice as she could manage.

"Helen, how are you doing?" Helen frantically hit the side button to lower the volume as Jack's stage voice boomed from the phone.

"Fine."

"I just wanted to thank you for agreeing to get a lawyer so quickly to look over the divorce papers. "

"My pleasure."

Oblivious to Helen's sarcasm, Jack plowed ahead. "Everything is going super well here. It's just that, well, we have a few people who specifically want to work with you." Helen's headache suddenly eased. "Brittany and I were wondering if you might be interested in taking on a few clients. As many or as few as you want. Of course, it's totally up to you. But there's no reason we can't still work together, and I understand from Kim that you're not working at all."

Helen saw red. *No reason we can't still work together*?? *You mean I should just forget the fact that you cheated on me right under my nose?* Helen was livid.

"Jack, it will be a cold day in hell before I ever work with you again. So let's just drop this right now."

"I wouldn't be too hasty, Helen. I don't see you staying in Poplar Point for long, and job opportunities for someone your age are pretty limited."

Helen's finger hovered over the red button. Bastard. "Well actually, just last night I heard about an opportunity here in Poplar Point. Turns out my business skills just might still be in demand."

Jack laughed. "Business skills in Poplar Point? That's a joke. What're you gonna do—dash out and open a knitting shop?"

"Jack, you really are a jerk."

"Seriously, though, what could you possibly find to do in Poplar Point, and why would you want to stay there anyway?"

"Oh, did you forget? Our daughter and son-in-law and two grandchildren live in Poplar Point. You should check them out sometime before Emma and Ben are grown and gone, just like Kim. I'm not making that mistake again."

Jack hesitated. "Right. I just never pegged you for granny of the year. So, what's this business opportunity?"

"Nothing I care to share with you."

"Well, just let me know when you come to your senses."

"And just why would I do that? Been good talking to you, Jack."

Helen jabbed at the red button, finally disconnecting on her third try.

Good God, was she seriously thinking about a marijuana store? Helen had been too upset to sleep and so, after several cups of strong coffee, had stayed up late reading about the cannabis industry. She couldn't believe the amount of money the industry was generating and the kinds of people and businesses that were investing. Things had come a long way since Helen's memories of high school when a group of sketchy losers had bought bags of homegrown marijuana from the local ice cream man.

Not that Helen had ever partaken. Jack had adamantly opposed the use of marijuana. That is until Brittany came along and Jack transformed into his new younger and hipper self. But what did *she* actually think about it? Honestly, she didn't know.

Helen leaned back in her chair, folding her arms and resting her chin on one fist. The more she looked back at her life, the more she realized that since she had fallen under the spell of Jack Roberts, every deeply held belief, every preference, and every major life decision had been his. Her mother had been a distant and somewhat cold presence in her life, and her father, while affectionate enough when the two of them were together, had always been at the office or away on business. But then along came Jack, captain of the football team, president of the church youth fellowship, and popular high school sweetheart. He had filled a void in Helen's life that she hadn't even known existed. Helen had followed him to Boston after high school, and they had married as soon as they graduated from college. Jack had made their career decisions, chosen their houses, picked out the clubs they joined and who they socialized with. Jack's political opinions were Helen's. Jack's taste in clothes, food, and wine dictated Helen's choices.

Helen felt somewhat shaken. She hadn't done an inventory like this in way too long. Was she really this shallow? Helen had always thought of herself as strong and independent—as a leader. But Jack's betrayal had crushed her. Who was she really, and what did she want now that Jack was no longer calling the shots? What she would give to show Jack that she could be successful without him—that she didn't need him after all.

CHAPTER 7

ALICE

Alice walked into Millie's Bakery and Café several days later, setting the café door's Open sign swinging jauntily on its red string. Though the shop was nearly invisible to tourists, it was the true beating heart of Poplar Point. Nothing happened in the town that wasn't planned, discussed, and later recounted at Millie's. This morning, the familiar smells of baking bread and brewing coffee folded Alice in their embrace. Millie was not only a gracious host but also a fabulous baker. Alice noticed that about half the small round wood tables in the front window were occupied by customers, most of whom she recognized.

Alice grabbed a seat near the window and stared nostalgically out at the town's small business district, marveling at how little it had changed since the days of her childhood. Many of the shops were the same, so far fending off the big box stores that blighted so many of America's streets. Alice felt a rush of affection for the town.

Not that there weren't problems here. Every year a bit more paint peeled off the storefronts and the sidewalks sported new cracks that tripped up even the most careful pedestrians. The explosion of tourism and influx of the super–wealthy with their private planes, expensive cars and fancy houses had largely by–passed Poplar Point, which was just fine with its long–time residents. To Alice and the other old–timers, Poplar Point was still perfect—a quiet, quaint town, with large yards and beautiful gardens, and the smell of the sea in the air. But even she had to admit, the town badly needed a shot in the arm. Its population had been slowly declining—and definitely graying as its center of gravity tilted a bit more every year in the direction of the Live Strong Senior Center run by Timmy Wentworth.

"Good morning, Alice." A deep bass voice interrupted Alice's reverie, reminding her of a well–tuned foghorn. *Oh, shit. Reverend Larson.* Though his rich baritone voice seemed to many in his congregation to reflect a divine presence, Alice just found it irritating.

Alice suspiciously eyed the clipboard in the Reverend's hands, then summoned a greeting. "Hello, Brendan. Where have you been hiding out? I haven't seen you for a while." *Ha!* thought Alice. *A little offense is always the best defense.* She was beyond tired of the Reverend's pressure tactics to attend church. It just wasn't her thing, particularly now that he had gone all evangelical in an effort to fill the church again. She'd be damned if he was going to make her feel guilty.

Brendan's eyes bored into hers, pinning her to the spot where she sat. Predictably, he launched into yet another moralistic pronouncement. "As you know, Alice, the town will vote on Poplar Point's future in the next couple of weeks. On behalf of Save Our Children, I'm gathering signatures on a petition to keep Poplar Point cannabis–free. We're hoping to collect the signatures of most of the people in town to ensure that we stop any store from locating here." He thrust the clipboard in her direction.

This was a set–up. Alice was sure Brendan knew she was a habitual user, and on top of that, a libertarian with vague religious beliefs tending toward Buddhism. She took a deep breath.

"Um ... I think you know I'm on the other side, Brendan. I don't see how having a store in Poplar Point could hurt. Lots of people use cannabis already, and their money is going who knows where. This way, Poplar Point would at least benefit from the tax revenue." Alice sensed she wasn't making any headway. "And you never know, the vibe around here just might improve." She laughed, although a bit hollowly.

Brendan did not smile. He held the clipboard closer to her. Alice could see it contained quite a number of signatures already. Wait, was that Helen's name? Alice didn't have her reading glasses on, but she was pretty sure she could make out one of the signatures.

"Alice, your position is extremely irresponsible. Using marijuana to get high is clearly not consistent with being a good citizen or a decent Christian."

Brendan was certainly on his high horse today. Alice knew that underneath his bluster and Christian uber–certainty, he had a kind heart, but she resented it when he spoke to her as though she were a child.

"Well, it *is* legal now, Brendan, so the church may need to rethink its position."

"Never, Alice. The Bible tells us that God's laws, not man's, determine right from wrong. And do you honestly want the town to make money from the addictions and illnesses of its weakest citizens?! And imagine the effect on the town's young people if they get easy access to drugs. The next thing you know, they'll be standing on the street corner vaping, and hard drugs will follow close behind." Alice felt like kicking herself. She knew better than to get into a debate with Brendan. "Here's a brochure listing the many health problems associated with marijuana. Even if you reject the moral arguments, you should read it. It could save your life." Brendan glared at her, his thick eyebrows knitted together and his heavy–lipped mouth turned down at the corners, leaving no doubt of his deep disapproval. Alice maintained eye contact for as long as she could, then took the brochure without thinking. When she tried to hand it back, Brendan was already striding away, another potential convert in his sights.

Alice dropped the brochure on the table. If Brendan controlled the narrative, Poplar Point's shot at a pot shop would definitely go up in smoke.

"Alice, there you are!" Alice turned to see Millie striding up to the table, her dark blond hair pinned up as usual in a loose bun and flour coating her white apron. She bent down to give Alice a quick hug and peck on the cheek. "I see the Reverend caught you before you even had a chance to get settled. He's been out and about all week threatening hell and damnation if the town gets swept up in reefer madness."

"What do you think, Millie?"

"I think a cannabis store might be just what this old town needs. About half the shops here are barely hanging on. You have no idea how much everyone is struggling."

Millie stepped away to ring up a croissant and a go cup of joe for a customer, but circled right back. "As near as I can tell, this is going to be a knock–down, drag–out fight. But if the town decides to allow a cannabis store, it could be a fabulous business opportunity for someone and a life-saver for the town. Whoops—gotta go. Can't keep the customers waiting. I'll get Rose to grab you some coffee and I'll catch you later." Millie glanced back over her shoulder at Alice. "Have you met Rose yet?" Alice shook her head. "You'll love her!"

Millie rushed back to the register, the smell of pastry lingering behind her. What a beautiful woman, Alice thought. And what I wouldn't give to have her talent as an artist! Alice gazed around the café, taking in Millie's latest artwork on the worn brick walls. It had been a great day for Poplar Point when Millie had come to town ten years ago and bought the old café. Millie had been a breath of fresh air. She and Alice had hit it off right away, and, despite the difference in their ages, Alice regarded Millie as her closest friend. Every once in a while, though, Alice realized how little she knew of Millie's life before she came to Poplar Point. Millie could hardly be described as quiet, but she had a way of smoothly redirecting the conversation whenever it began to cut close to her earlier years.

A couple of minutes later, a tall, slightly harried–looking young woman walked up to Alice's table, notepad and pencil in hand. Rose was not classically beautiful, but Alice was struck by her thick lustrous dark hair, her large expressive eyes with their gorgeous lashes, and her generous, sensuous mouth. No doubt she was going to be turning more than a few heads in town.

"Hi, I'm Rose Marchetti," she said with a friendly smile. "And you're Alice—right? I've heard so much about you from Millie."

Alice held out her hand. "It's nice to meet you, Rose, and welcome to Poplar Point."

Rose wiped some of the flour off her hand onto her apron and shook Alice's hand warmly. "Nice to meet you, too. Can I get you something?"

"Absolutely."

Alice watched Rose hurry off with her order. Millie had a way of befriending young women who needed a helping hand. She wondered what Rose's story was.

CHAPTER 8

ALICE

Alice had just settled comfortably into coffee and a muffin when her phone rang. She fumbled in her pocket, trying to silence it quickly. As she brought the phone to her ear, she glanced at the number. Unknown. Probably spam.

Alice thought about ignoring the call, but then answered with a slight note of suspicion in her voice. "Hello?"

"Alice? It's Helen."

Alice's eyebrows shot up. "Hi, Helen. How are you?"

"More than a little embarrassed, but otherwise fine. I do have to thank you for your help the other night. I don't know what came over me."

"No problem, Helen." Alice did feel some sympathy for Helen, even if she had gotten a certain enjoyment out of seeing Helen laid out on the sidewalk. "What can I do for you?"

"Well, I've been thinking about that article in the paper and everything Bear said when I was at your house. You know, about business opportunities around opening a marijuana store in Poplar Point. I think we should get together and talk about it."

Even though Alice had noticed Helen's sudden interest in a marijuana store when the topic of money had come up, she was still stunned. Had Bear gotten to Helen despite Alice's warning that it wasn't a good idea?

"I know this must seem a little strange, Alice, coming from me. I understand we weren't the best of friends growing up, but honestly, that was a long time ago. Maybe it's time to put the past behind us."

Oh, no—was Helen actually thinking of staying in Poplar Point? Helen, Alice wanted to say, *it's not just that we weren't best friends, we positively disliked each other, and I can't imagine it would be any different now. Look at us! We have nothing in common. Our goals and value systems are totally inconsistent. In high school, you and your friends treated me like dirt. And your mother's obvious dislike for my mother didn't help. Besides, you always hated Poplar Point!*

But Alice thought of Bear. She kept her thoughts to herself, at least for the moment. "Well, it never hurts to talk. But you do understand, Helen, what we're talking about here. About opening a store that sells marijuana?? You sure you're comfortable with that?"

There was a pause. "Well, I'd be open to learning more about it."

"And didn't I see your name on Brendan's petition?!"

There was a longer pause. "Oh, that. Yes, I signed it. But I actually have been thinking about the store idea. I just didn't want him to know. I needed to do some research. Do you have some time in the next few days for me to share what I've found?"

"Sure," Alice said hesitantly. "Why don't you just text me when you're ready to talk."

"Will do. Thanks, Alice."

Alice placed her phone back in the pocket of her voluminous sweater and picked up her coffee. Well, that was unexpected, to put it mildly. And most unlike Helen—at least the Helen of forty years ago. But then again, what with Jack divorcing her and all, Helen was undoubtedly not at her best. Once her head cleared, she would surely reconsider.

Alice watched the cars slowly traversing Main Street, pulling in and out of the brightly designated parking spaces. If she was honest with herself, Poplar Point, now in its later years, was definitely in need of a major face–lift. Alice unconsciously touched her chin, picked up the check and dropped several dollar bills on the table. She glanced back over her shoulder as she walked out the door. "Thanks, Millie. I'll be back."

As Alice stepped out of the café, she spotted Brendan's wife, Faye, standing by the curb, obviously waiting for her husband. She was conservatively dressed in a light wool skirt and sweater; a cardboard box stuffed with brochures lay at her feet. Alice hesitated, but then walked toward her, a smile on her face. "Faye, how are you?"

Faye rolled her eyes. "Fuckin' bored out of my mind." Alice made a conscious effort to tug her eyebrows back down. "Saint Brendan is off on another crusade to save the world. Why, this time I guess he's out to save the world from the likes of you. How do you like that, Alice?"

"Not much, to be honest, Faye."

Faye laughed heartily, attracting the attention of other passersby on the street. "You always were honest to a fault, Alice! Honestly, I'm rather glad that at least for now he has a cause other than saving my sorry soul."

"Well, I'll do my best to keep him occupied for a while, Faye. A lot of us will not be seeing eye to eye with him on this one."

Good God, thought Alice. The rumors must be true. Faye had been away at an unusual number of religious retreats over the past few years, and the word around town was that she was actually drying out or recovering from some sort of mental breakdown. It was hard to believe this was the same lovely young woman who had arrived in Poplar Point so many years ago, madly in love with Brendan and eager to become a part of the community. But Alice knew a little of their struggles in the early years when they were trying unsuccessfully to get pregnant. And Brendan, with his over–sized ego, was undoubtedly not an easy man to live with.

As Alice turned toward her car, she heard Faye call out behind her. "I'll be praying for you!" Faye continued to laugh.

Alice wondered exactly what Faye would be praying for.

CHAPTER 9

BEAR

Bear pulled up to his mother's house and was surprised to see a BMW in the driveway where he usually parked his pickup. His curiosity piqued, Bear sauntered in the side door and was instantly gratified to see a pot of chili warming on the old iron stove. Helen's and Alice's voices carried clearly from the living room into the kitchen. *Damn,* thought Bear, *sounds like something's got them wound up.*

"Alice, I've been doing quite a bit of research since we last spoke. First off, it's not clear to me the town will vote to legalize the sale of recreational marijuana here. The split among townships that have already voted is about 50/50, and Brendan has stirred up a lot of public opinion. But even if the town is persuaded, opening a store or dispensary or whatever you want to call it is much more complicated than I would have thought."

"Well, that's kind of what I expected."

Helen acted as though she had not heard Alice. "There are tons of legal and regulatory hoops to jump through and some real practical problems. Then there's the product. You wouldn't believe how many ways there are to use marijuana now! Nobody just rolls joints anymore. You can get them already rolled for you. And there are edibles, concentrates, crazy things called dabs and moon rocks—lots of things. Why, I even saw a picture of a store online with a drive-through window, and in some places people deliver to your door just like ordering a pizza from Domino's!

"To be honest, I was ready to give up on the whole idea. It's just too much. But then I had a brainstorm. A year ago, I sold a house to a wealthy business entrepreneur who specializes in franchises. You do know what a franchise is, right? Like McDonald's?"

Bear winced. He knew how much his mother hated being talked down to.

"Yes, Helen, I know what a franchise is."

Once again Helen seemed not to have heard Alice. "So I called him and sure enough, he knew exactly the right guy. Someone named Matt Jacobson. Apparently, he spent years working in the medical marijuana industry in Boston and now runs a franchise operation for recreational marijuana stores. Can you imagine? Anyway, I made an appointment for you, Bear, and me to meet with him next week."

"What?!? You what?!?" Alice sputtered. "Don't you think you should have talked to us first? The three of us haven't even decided if we all want to do this!"

Uh–oh, thought Bear. Even more than being talked down to, he knew how negatively his mom reacted to being pressured.

"I know, Alice. But we aren't committing ourselves to anything. Just gathering information."

"I get that, Helen, but still, you'll have to admit this whole idea seems a little strange. Good God, have you ever even smoked a joint?"

"Well, no. But then again, I never owned any multimillion–dollar houses, and I sold a lot of them! Bear was right. When you look at what we each bring to the table, I think we can do this. But we need to put aside our differences and approach this professionally, like mature adults." Bear could just picture the self–satisfied look on Helen's face.

Alice didn't rise to the bait. "But first the town has to decide to allow a pot business to open here. I understand the Board of Selectmen has announced its opposition to the idea. And I was quite taken aback by the number of signatures Brendan Larson has already collected. Speaking of which, what the hell, Helen? I still can't believe you signed that petition!"

"It's not that simple, Alice. Everyone in town knows you've smoked pot since you were in middle school. And then you and Arlo moved to that commune outside of town for a while before you got married. Nothing like advertising you do drugs and don't care what normal people think."

Bear could sense his mother's rising anger all the way from the kitchen, but she held her tongue while Helen continued, oblivious to her condescending tone. "It's not like that for me. I have a certain reputation to uphold. I'm thinking I could be a 'silent' partner. I can work with Matt or whoever is doing the business side of things. You and Bear have all the connections and can be the face of the business."

"I don't know about that, Helen. I'm not saying I think any of this is a good idea, but if we did try something like this, together, I think we would have to be real partners. I'm not willing to take a lot of risk by putting up some money and providing a place for a shop while you make all the decisions."

"No, no ... that's not what I mean. Let's think about the upcoming Town Meeting, for example. I can do a little more research and write up something you and Bear can take to the businesspeople in town, explaining how this can boost profits and employment opportunities for everyone. You—and Bear—can reach out to the store owners and to other potential supporters who I wouldn't know at all."

Bear perked up. Helen was right. He and his mom knew a bunch of people who would probably love to have a pot shop in town. Indeed, Bear had procured weed for at least half the town leaders at some time in their lives.

Bear began mentally adding to his list of all the things they could do to make the town come around.

As Bear dug into a bowl of chili, the voices in the living room died down. A few minutes later, the front porch door slapped shut and Alice walked into the kitchen. She looked worn down and frustrated.

"Ma," said Bear between spoonfuls, "I couldn't help but overhear your conversation with Helen. I think this could be a partnership made in heaven."

"Honestly, honey?" Alice sounded upset.

She sat down heavily in one of the cane chairs around the sturdy but stained wood table. "Good God, Bear. I'm not sure you fully appreciate my history with Helen. Helen has looked down her nose at me her whole life. We are as different as two people can be, and we have disliked each other for years. Why, just tonight, even when she wanted something from me, she insulted me multiple times and didn't even realize it."

"I get it, Ma. She did come across a bit like a steamroller."

"A bit? That's putting it mildly. Then there's the whole thing with our mothers. Helen's mother hated Grandma. Wouldn't even speak to her if they passed on the street. I asked Grandma why so many times, but she refused to talk about it—just ignored the whole thing. At my age, I'm just not sure I want to get involved with Helen and put myself in a situation that could be upsetting for me."

"I know, I know, Ma. But this is business. We're not talkin' about you and Helen becoming best friends or anything. It would be different if you thought Helen was dishonest or lazy or something. Let's take things one step at a time here. We should at least explore whether we can work this out." Bear got up and dished up some chili in a bowl for his mom. "Here, eat some of this dee–licious chili. I have tons of ideas for how we can steal old Reverend Larson's thunder and convince the town to allow a store. This could be a good thing for us, Ma—and good for the town."

Bear gave his mom his most confident and winning smile and pushed ahead with his latest ideas for a store. He had to make his mom see what an opportunity this was.

CHAPTER 10

BEAR

As *JEOPARDY* ENDED LATER THAT evening and yet another commercial for Viagra blasted from the ancient TV, Bear hoisted himself out of his sunken spot on the old couch. "Thanks for dinner, Ma. It's time for me to get on my way."

Alice rocked herself out of her chair and gave her only child a tight hug. "I'm so glad you stopped by, Bear. It was good that you got to hear what Helen had to say—and how she said it. But don't you worry—I'll keep an open mind. We'll figure this out."

As Bear headed out the front door to his truck, he stopped in the yard, hands on hips, and gazed up with satisfaction at the black sky studded with millions of icy cold sparkling stars. Maybe he was finally catching a break.

Everyone, even his own mom most of the time, assumed life was just hunky–dory for good old Bear, when, in fact, he often felt like a total failure. He had been content for a time skipping the college train to work with his dad in the store, but all that had ended one disastrous afternoon. Since then, jobs had been scarce and hard to keep. Did people really think he was happy living in an old trailer outside of town, driving his beat–up pickup, and mooching meals off his mom?

His record in the romance department was equally depressing. What could be harder than watching the girl you've loved since high school go off and marry someone else and then move into town?

Bear decided to stop for a nightcap at Sharky's. He drove into town and parked on a dark side street, hoping the police wouldn't see his truck and boot it again for all his unpaid tickets. As he climbed out on the driver's side, a figure jumped out of the shadows, knocking him to the ground. Before he could catch his breath, a large man was kneeling on his chest with the front of his flannel shirt gripped tightly in his fist.

"Well, who do we have here? Just who I was about to go looking for."

Bear stared into the cold, dark eyes of Marty Doyle, his nemesis since high school when Bear had taken "Marty's" position on the Poplar Point High School football team.

"Where's the two thousand bucks you owe me?" Marty tightened his grip. "I told you to pay up. Now I'm getting pressured, and it's your fault, asshole."

Bear's relationship with Marty had been complicated for a long time. Bear had been buying weed off Marty for years, both for his personal consumption and for some low–level deals of his own. Somehow, the money had gotten away from him these past several months. But Bear hadn't been too worried. Usually, he could work things out with Marty who, despite his obsession with body building, shied away from violence which might provoke the interest of the local cops.

As Marty's chokehold eased a tad, Bear managed to croak, "Ah, come on, Marty. You know I'm good for it."

Marty pulled his fist off Bear's shirt and let it fly, punching Bear straight in the face. Bear was totally gobsmacked as blood gushed from his nose.

"What the hell, Marty?!?"

"You don't want to mess with me, Bear. I'm not a small–time operator anymore, selling a little dope on the side for a few extra bucks. I've got people I answer to now. This is serious, Bear. Pay up or you better believe the next time you see me will be worse." Marty stood and followed his threat with a swift kick to Bear's gut.

Stunned, Bear retched as he felt the burn of salty tears mixing with the blood still flowing from his nose. How had he let Marty get the jump on him? And what the hell was going on?

As Marty swaggered down the sidewalk, quickly blending back into the shadows, Bear stared up at the sky again. It was still black and filled with twinkling stars. But this time, Bear felt nothing but dread. He had heard Marty had hooked up with a larger operation out of Fall River and now dealt everything from weed to meth to fentanyl. Clearly, the game was changing—and so was Marty.

While Bear lay uncomfortably on his back trying to catch his breath, he heard the click clack of high heels clattering off the sidewalk. Within seconds, two voices, a man's and a woman's, drifted in his direction.

"Kim, you are such a pain in the ass. All I hear is bitch, bitch, bitch. And work has taken over your life. You'd think you were President of the United States the way you carry on. Why don't you just go on home? Put the kids to bed or something and give your mom a break. I'm going to Sharky's—without you. I need a little fun."

Oh, shit. Bear struggled to sit up before Kim and Kevin spotted him, but the pain in his side sent him back onto one elbow.

Kim and Kevin continued down the sidewalk, now in sullen silence. When they spotted a large figure some twenty feet ahead trying to push himself to his feet, they slowed, approaching cautiously. Suddenly, Kim shot forward.

"Bear! What happened? Are you hurt? Do you need help? Should I call your mother?"

Bear winced as he caught Kevin's look of unconcealed disgust.

"Kim, I'll be home later. Don't bother waiting up. Don't get carried away playing Florence Nightingale or anything." Kevin snickered as he stepped around Bear and then quickened his pace as he headed toward town.

"I'm OK, Kim. I just need to get back to my truck."

"But what happened, Bear? Shouldn't you go to the police? Or the emergency room?"

"Nah. It's no big deal. Just a bloody nose." Bear's eyes rose to meet Kim's as he hauled himself to his feet. Whoa. In Bear's eyes, she was as beautiful as ever. Then Bear took a closer look. "Kim, have you been crying? What's wrong?"

Kim clumsily brushed the tears off her cheeks.

"It's Kevin, isn't it?" Some heat crept into Bear's voice.

"Why would you say that, Bear?"

"I thought I heard you two arguing as you walked toward me." In fact, Bear had more reason than that to suspect all was not well in paradise. For months now, Kevin had been hitting on the waitresses at Sharky's, and rumor had it he had finally scored. *Asshole.* Didn't Kevin know what he had in Kim? It seemed like only yesterday Kim and Kevin had been the toast of the town, the perfect couple.

Even in the dim light of the street lamp, Bear saw Kim's cheeks redden.

"It's no big deal," Kim said hastily. "We're fine. Here, let me help you." Kim handed Bear a wad of Kleenex from her purse.

"Thanks. Listen, Kim—I know we haven't seen much of each other for a long time, but we will always be friends. If you ever need someone to talk to, you know where to find me. I'm a good listener, and I keep things to myself."

Kim smiled wanly. "I know, Bear. I haven't forgotten. You better be careful or I just might take you up on your offer. I could use a friend about now, and there aren't many people I can talk to."

"Any time, Kim." Bear watched as Kim turned and walked away—click clack click clack. Seeing her so unhappy broke Bear's heart. She really deserved better. Bear headed for his truck. What a night.

CHAPTER 11

ALICE

"Welcome! Come on in and take a seat! I'm Matt Jacobson." Matt walked around the large oval conference table, taking care to give each of them a firm handshake and personal greeting. Alice noticed Matt held Helen's hand a fraction of a second longer than hers or Bear's. *Oh, for Pete's sake. What am I doing?* Alice scolded herself lightly for being so critical.

Alice glanced out the tall windows at the skyline and the water beyond, then took a seat in a sleek black leather chair next to Bear. It had been years since Alice had been in the "big city," and the traffic and general air of decay made her appreciate Poplar Point more than ever.

Matt seemed like a nice enough guy, though perhaps a bit of a salesman. Tall and fit in an obviously expensive suit, he had a full head of dark hair heavily salted with grey. He was older than Alice had expected, but still exuded a certain youthfulness. Alice was secretly relieved they wouldn't end up taking orders from a bunch of millennials who would inevitably treat her like she was past her expiration date.

Helen, who had worn her red power suit for the occasion, grabbed the seat next to Matt. She was clearly thrilled to be back in meeting–mode. As soon as the introductions were over, she and Matt were talking a mile a minute in a lingo that made Alice feel like she had just dropped into a different planet—market surveys, rates of return, branding. Matt met every comment of Helen's with a nod, a smile, and a compliment. Helen was eating it up. *Is she so starved for attention and positive reinforcement she doesn't even realize how Matt is playing her?* thought Alice. *Oh, dear.* Alice chastised herself a second time.

Next, Alice focused on Bear, who was also actively taking part in the conversation. Bear confidently described for Matt the challenges facing the town, the interest among the local farmers in growing marijuana, and the potential market. Alice was proud of him; Helen appeared to be favorably impressed, too.

Alice knew she was being uncharacteristically quiet. True, this meeting was a little out of her realm of experience. But she wasn't feeling intimidated; she just had nothing to add to the conversation. Besides, she knew that sometimes you learn more by listening and observing.

As the meeting wrapped up, Matt's gaze traveled around the table, landing on Alice. "From what I've heard this afternoon, Poplar Point sounds like a perfect spot for a recreational cannabis dispensary. Alice, it's fantastic you already have extensive contacts in the town and surrounding area, plus an ideal location."

Matt gave Alice his best smile, then paused to look at each of them. "You can certainly try going forward on your own. But if you decide to operate as a franchise, we bring a ton of experience in the cannabis industry to the table, as well as a proven business model. How about if I send a proposal to you by the end of next week?"

Helen and Bear readily agreed; Alice's face remained neutral. She wasn't about to get rushed into something she wasn't even sure she wanted to do. Besides, the fees Matt had quoted struck her as totally outrageous.

As the meeting was about to wrap up, Alice suddenly spoke up. "Matt, before we go, do you mind telling us how you got into the marijuana business?"

Helen and Bear looked at Alice curiously, wondering where she was going with this. Matt was unfazed. "My older brother developed glaucoma when he was young. The prescription drugs that were available at the time didn't work well for him. There was at least some anecdotal evidence that pot helped alleviate the pressure in the eyes that results from glaucoma, so I joined the fight for legalization of medical marijuana. Honestly, it wasn't how I envisioned spending my life, but I have now been involved in the cannabis industry for thirty years in one way or another."

"I'm sorry to hear about your brother, Matt. How's he doing?" Alice was genuinely concerned.

"Well, cannabis didn't turn out to be the miracle we had all hoped for, but it did help. He has lost some of his sight now, but better treatments are coming out all the time."

Although Alice felt a little embarrassed, she forged ahead. "And tell us a bit more about you, Matt." Alice gave him an encouraging smile. "Are you married? Do you have kids? Or is work your whole life?"

"I'm divorced. My ex–wife put up with my work with medical marijuana even though there wasn't much money in it. But when the business began moving into recreational marijuana, she wasn't on board." Both Matt and Alice noted the disapproving looks Helen and Bear were shooting in Alice's direction. "Actually, this is not a bad conversation to have. You've probably encountered this by now, but there are a lot of people out there who won't approve of what you are doing. A huge amount of negative stereotyping and judging goes on. You have to be sure you're willing to live with that and all that comes with it."

"Honestly, that's something I've dealt with my whole life. But with a few notable exceptions, Poplar Point's a pretty comfortable place in that respect." Alice noticed Bear nodding. "Thanks for being upfront with us, Matt."

After handshakes all around and promises to be in touch, Alice, Helen and Bear made their way to the elevator. "What the hell was that, Alice?" Helen gave Alice a hard stare.

"Come on, Helen, if we're thinking of going into business with this guy and paying him such exorbitant fees, I want to know a little more about him."

"You don't think I would have set this up without having done my due diligence, do you?"

"Your do what?"

Helen snorted. "I've already checked him out, Alice. In a business arrangement, you don't start off by asking someone if they're married! That's like asking a woman if she's pregnant!"

"It is not! I'm not asking if he's planning on taking divorce leave! I just want to know something about him as a person."

"Seriously, Alice. How would you have felt if he had asked you if you were married?"

"I wouldn't have minded. How would *you* have felt if he had asked you? I would guess downright excited based on how you played up to him!"

"I did not!"

Bear groaned as they rode down the elevator and entered the lobby. "OK, ladies. How about you two wait here while I go get the truck?" Alice and Helen nodded, not taking their eyes off each other as Bear made a beeline out the door.

"By the way, Alice, Matt's business reputation is stellar, but his personal reputation is more, well, colorful. Apparently, he's known as quite the ladies' man and he's had more than a few affairs with some high–rolling women around the city, including while he was married. His wife came with piles of old money, which explains their extravagant lifestyle while he was busy promoting medical marijuana."

"Helen, if you knew all this, why did you play along with him? Couldn't you see he was buttering you up?"

"Of course I could! I'm not planning on jumping in bed with him. If he thinks I'm an easy mark, that's all the better for us."

What Alice would have given to wipe the smug expression off Helen's face.

On the drive home, Helen was on a roll. It was as though the decision to open a store together had already been made, and now her brain was on fire with random thoughts about every detail of the venture.

"I liked the different layouts he showed us in his presentation, although the mobile model is definitely what we want, assuming we can get good employees. I picture it a lot like the Apple store. You know, all chrome and white, with cool lighting. Maybe some leather swivel barstools at the counters. Kind of like the ones at the make–up counter at Neiman's. And speaking of make–up, I love the idea of all the related beauty products and lotions they're starting to make with cannabis or CBD. Bubble bath bombs, sleeping masks, even edibles for pets. And all those cute little pipes. And cookbooks for munchies. Munchies! Imagine!"

Alice had had it. "Helen! Stop! This is not Boston or Las Vegas or LA or wherever it is you think you are. This is Poplar Point we're talking about. Nobody wants an Apple store or fancy swivel stools you can't even lean back in. This is exactly what I was afraid of. You coming busting in, full of your big city ideas, and dictating what everybody's going to do!"

Helen looked surprised. "I'm sorry, Alice. I know I can sound a little bossy at times, but really—I'm not trying to dictate."

You know you can sound a little *bossy?* thought Alice.

"It was just so much more than I expected. I guess I got carried away. I don't mean to cut anyone out. What's your vision, Alice?"

"My *vision*? This is not some magic mushroom trip and I'm not Alice in Wonderland, Helen."

"Ma, Ma," interjected Bear as he steered the truck through Boston's usual horrific traffic. "Come on. We've all got ideas, and if we put them together, we might just come up with something beautiful."

Good grief, thought Alice. *Was I looking the other way or something when they were handing out the gummy samples?*

Alice took a calming breath. "Well, OK. I guess I was picturing something a little more homey, more retro. Solid wood display cases, old posters on the walls, lots of green plants, tee–shirts for sale, a yoga studio in the back. Stuff like that."

Helen rolled her eyes.

"I saw that, Helen! That is precisely what I'm talking about. You've been treating me like I'm stupid since we were in high school!"

"That's ridiculous. I never paid any attention to you in high school."

"You mean you and your friends couldn't be bothered with the riff raff like my friends and me."

"Ma! Helen! That's enough!" Bear was clearly struggling for a way out of this. "You both have great ideas, drawn from your somewhat different life experiences and natural proclivities."

Humph ... since when did Bear start talking like this? Alice stared out the window.

Bear rolled on. "I think we're all agreed we've got the room to have a comfortable space as opposed to just a cold dispensary. When we put everything together and pick the best from both your worlds, we'll get it *exactly* right."

More like we'll have a real mess on our hands, like trying to mix oil and water. Alice shot Helen a squinty side glance to make sure she knew she wasn't buying this horseshit.

"For now," Bear continued, "we need to decide whether we want to move forward and if so, whether we want to work with Matt. Then we have to figure out how we're going to persuade the town not to ban the sale of marijuana and to grant us a permit."

Helen perked back up. "Well, I've been thinking about that, Bear. I totally agree with Matt that we need to get organized right away. What was the franchise name he mentioned? Poplar Point Safe Access, I think. I like it, don't you? It would be a great name for our campaign and our store." Helen continued blithely on before either Bear or Alice had a chance to comment. "I've already written up some talking points for each of you."

Talking points? Now she thinks she has to tell us what to say? Alice frowned.

"And I'm about done with some promotional materials you can hand out. We can identify different demographics, tailor our promotional materials to their interests, and then divide them between you two and any other volunteers we get to achieve maximum market saturation."

As they finally pulled into the driveway at Alice's, Bear switched off the engine and turned to look at them both. "OK. Let's do it! Let's go inside and have a drink to celebrate!"

Helen brightened at the mention of a drink and she and Bear headed for the door, while Alice followed a few steps behind. This was starting to sound like a done deal, whether she liked it or not.

As Alice settled in her chair in the living room, she gazed out the window at the old elm in the yard. What had she gotten herself into? And why was she reacting so negatively? Really, what did she know anyway? She definitely had to leave time tonight for some thinking and meditation. She could hear Timmy now: she needed to embrace this moment, her life, just as it is. She took a few calming breaths. Embracing the prospect of working with Helen was a tall order, but Alice knew she had to try if that's what it took to support Bear.

CHAPTER 12

BEAR

THE LAST BUGS OF THE unusually warm fall splatted against the windshield of the dirty truck as Bear drove the winding state highway. The sun was already dipping below the horizon, its pink and orange glow slowly fading and turning the now resting fields a lingering gold.

The last few days had taken a toll on Bear as he, Helen, and his mom began to navigate the choppy waters of their emerging partnership. Helen had been busily composing lists and assigning relevant reading, while his mom had fluctuated between staying stubbornly mute and then interjecting pointed, thoughtful questions that often stopped them cold. Bear tried to keep his head down, but often felt like he was being whacked back and forth by two rumbling powerhouses—one in pressed slacks and a neat blouse, the other in loosely gathered tops and pants with well–worn Tevas on her feet. Hence, the pressing need for a cold beer with his best friend, Jed Dawson.

Jed and his wife Chrissie had not grown up around Poplar Point, but Bear and Jed had hit it off the moment they crossed paths at the vegetable co–op in town. In Bear's estimation, Jed and Chrissie represented the very best of their generation's back–to–the–land movement.

Suddenly Bear's foot hit the brakes. The truck screeched to a stop, a cloud of dust billowing behind it. *What the hell?* A large red "For Sale" sign was staked near the road in Jed's front field.

The truck lurched forward as Bear turned sharply into the narrow dirt road leading to Jed and Chrissie's farmhouse. He saw the lights come on in the house and then, out of the corner of his eye, caught movement near the half–falling down barn. Bear drove to the end of the drive and jumped from the cab as soon as the truck came to a stop.

"Jed, is that your For Sale sign by the road? What the fuck?"

Jed was cleaning some tools in the barn doorway. For the first time, Bear noticed the worry lines creasing his forehead.

Jed looked up, a half–smile tugging at the corners of his mouth. He dropped the rag in his hand and started across the stubbly yard to the front porch of the old farmhouse. "Come on, I sure could use a beer."

Bear walked into the sparsely furnished living room with Jed and immediately noticed the stacks of what looked like bills piled on the old oak dining table. How long had they been there, and why hadn't he noticed?

Jed reappeared a minute later, a bottle of Sam Adams Summer Ale in each hand. He motioned Bear to a chair and they both settled, legs stretched out. Bear took a hefty swig of his beer and wiped the back of his hand across his mouth.

"Where's Chrissie?"

"Puttin' Caleb to bed so we need to keep it down. He just hit the terrible two's, so bedtime's intense around here." Jed took a deep pull on his beer.

"So, what gives, Jed?"

Jed looked down at the bottle held in his hands. "Sorry, Bear. I didn't want to tell you but Chrissie and I are thinkin' we just can't make a go of this place. We put out the sign to test the waters."

Bear put his beer down on the table and leaned back in his chair, looking up at the ceiling. "Whoa. I had no idea things were that bad."

"All the small farmers around here have been struggling for years, but last year was really hard. We're all having trouble making ends meet. I'm not sure any of us is gonna make it if we can't come up with a reliable cash crop we can grow year–round. When Chrissie and I decided to leave Cincinnati and try our hand at living sustainably off the land, we weren't planning on living in abject poverty."

"Yeah, I get that."

They sat in silence, two big strong guys looking like the weight of the world was on their shoulders. Bear felt terrible that he had been so oblivious.

Finally Bear spoke. "Actually, Jed, the timing's a little funny but I stopped by to talk to you about an idea that might help. Yesterday, my mom, Helen Newbold and I met with a guy named Matt Jacobson who Helen introduced us to. Do you know Helen?"

"Not really. Isn't she Kim West's mother?"

"Yeah. Well, she's back in town for a while. Seems she's getting divorced. And she's got a lot of business experience."

Jed listened with interest as Bear relayed their initial ideas for getting into the green gold rush by opening a marijuana store in Poplar Point and running it as a franchise of Matt's brand, Safe Access.

"Wow, so you're actually thinking about doin' this?"

"I think so. I think we'll all feel better if we're working with an outfit that already knows the business. Have you been following what's going on in town?"

"Hell, yeah. I think it's shaping up to be a real fight. A group of us farmers have been expecting this for a while. We've been getting together regularly and we're in the early stages of organizing ourselves as a co–op. That way, we can pool our resources and set up a large–scale cultivation operation if some marijuana stores open around here."

Bear's eyes lit up. "That's great, Jed! I think there's real potential here—for the growers, the processors, the retailers, really the whole town."

"I agree." Jed swept his arm across the table. "But even after pooling our resources, I don't know how the co–op will get enough financing to set up a large–scale operation. Around here, a substantial portion of the cultivation needs to be indoors. And that ain't cheap."

Chrissie tiptoed into the room. "Hey, Bear." She placed her hands on Jed's shoulders and whispered in his ear, "The little monster's asleep."

"Grab a beer and a chair, Chrissie. Bear's been filling me in on his latest ideas for opening a pot store in Poplar Point and a meeting he had in Boston."

As soon as Chrissie stepped back in from the kitchen, beer in hand, Bear summarized everything he had told Jed. "I have to tell you, though—it's a little strange between my mom and Helen. You wouldn't believe how complicated their relationship is."

"How so?" asked Chrissie.

"For one thing, they're constantly sniping at each other. If one says it's sunny outside, you can bet money the other will say it's cloudy. Just yesterday on the way back from Boston, my mom went off on a riff about how Helen treated her in high school. High school! Can you believe it? That was over 40 years ago! But I think it's more than that. Since I was really small, I always heard there was bad blood between Helen's mother and my mom's mother. I don't know why. No one would ever talk about it. Kim and I used to wonder about it, but neither of us could figure it out."

"You and Kim were friends?"

"Kind of a secret romance for a couple of summers in high school. Kim lived in Boston, but spent her summers in Poplar Point with her grandmother. Kim didn't have any friends here, and I was kind of a loner, so we ended up spending a lotta time together. But Kim always wanted to keep it quiet. I figured she didn't want her mother to know. Or maybe I wouldn't fit in with her cooler friends back in Boston. Anyway, every fall, Kim would head back to Boston, and we'd each pick up our old lives. Once we graduated, we didn't see each other much. Kim went on to BU and met Kevin, and she didn't spend a lot of time in Poplar Point until she and Kevin had kids and decided to move back here."

"Do I sense some heartbreak here, Bear?" asked Chrissie, raising a perfectly arched eyebrow.

Bear laughed. "Maybe some one–sided heartbreak. Anyway, to make it even weirder, Helen's all in with the marijuana store idea, but doesn't want anyone to know about her involvement. You've got to swear you won't tell anyone she's involved."

Jed scratched his head. "OK. And good luck with that!"

Bear looked searchingly at Jed and Chrissie. "Do you think you can hold off on selling while the town sorts this all out?"

Jed and Chrissie looked at each other. "Well, we haven't exactly had a crowd of interested buyers lining up at the door," Jed finally said. Chrissie nodded. "So, how do we make this happen?"

Bear breathed a sigh of relief. "Well, Matt thought we needed to start organizing right away. He has franchise stores operating in six states already and we think the name they used for the stores will play well here. Poplar Point Safe Access—don't you think that sounds pretty legit?"

"Absolutely," said Jed. "Our cultivation group is planning on getting together Thursday night. Why don't you join us, Bear, and fill everybody in on what you're thinking?"

"Sounds like a plan, Jed. How about I get us a private table at Millie's and we can all grab a beer?"

"Great idea! How about eight?"

Chrissie laughed. "This is not how I pictured our lives as small farmers, but I say let's get to work!"

As Bear walked back out to his truck an hour or so later, he was super excited. The prospect of working with Jed and the other local farmers, all of whom he knew, seemed like a perfect fit. But then suddenly, the enormity of the project they were taking on hit him, leaving him feeling momentarily overwhelmed. There was so much to do, and so many people who had a lot at stake. Bear was way outside his comfort zone, but he wanted this badly. He sure hoped he was up to it.

CHAPTER 13

BEAR

THURSDAY NIGHT ROLLED AROUND QUICKLY—BUT not quickly enough for Bear. Bear had his heart set on having Safe Access be a community enterprise where most of the marijuana was produced locally by small farmers, rather than purchased from big corporations headquartered somewhere else. Plus, he felt sure that having local farmers involved would be another persuasive point in their favor at the Town Meeting.

Bear arrived at the café a few minutes early. Millie had already set up a large round table in the back with pitchers of frothy cold beer awaiting the group's arrival.

"Millie, thanks so much for doing this."

"No problem, Bear. You know I'd do anything for you and your mom." She gave him a quick hug as she passed on her way back to the kitchen. Bear turned and watched a series of dirty old pick–ups pull up in front of the café. Jed and his friends came through the door, laughing and slapping each other on the back. Everyone greeted Bear warmly.

Some of the farmers were much like Jed and Chrissie—young transplants from other places who had moved back to the land. Other families had been in the area for generations.

After pouring the beer, Jed got right down to business. He began by explaining to Bear how the seven farms were in the process of incorporating as a co–op called Grow Zone that would grow cannabis both outside during the warmer months and inside year–round. Pooling their resources was the only way they could even begin to cover the huge start–up costs for an indoor operation. Careful not to mention Helen, Bear told the group about his and his mother's meeting with Matt and their plans for trying to open a Safe Access franchise.

"What do you think the chances are that the Town Meeting will approve a store here in Poplar Point, Bear?"

"It's still early to say, but I'm hopeful. There's a ton of work to be done, though; we need to explain to everyone how this benefits the town. We're gonna need some help."

"You got yourself some volunteers right here, Bear," said one of the younger women, and everyone nodded.

"Anyone else here been buttonholed by Reverend Larson yet?" asked another young farmer.

"Sure have. He's busy as a bee threatenin' hell and damnation."

"That's why we need to get organized right away," said Bear.

"Ya know, Bear," said Hal Jenkins, the oldest farmer in the group. "I've been waitin' for years for opportunity to come knockin', and I can hear it now. Can't wait to tell my boys who skedaddled for the city as soon as they got out of school. They're gonna get a good chuckle out of the fact that their old dad is now growing marijuana! But, hell, it sure beats scooping chicken shit for a livin'."

"Amen," everyone agreed.

"The only problem is the financing," Hal continued. "But we're workin' on it."

"I know the financing's a big challenge, Hal, but I'm hopin' Matt will have some ideas," said Bear. "If you're interested, I can try to arrange a meeting for you all with Matt." Everyone nodded.

As the group broke up, Bear noticed Millie lingering nearby. She'd been hanging around the table all night. Something felt off. When he looked around again after saying his good-byes, Millie was gone.

CHAPTER 14

MILLIE

Later that night, Millie climbed the steep stairs to the spacious apartment she lived in above the café. The walls were painted bold colors. Thick Persian rugs were scattered on the polished dark wood floors, and her artwork covered every wall. This was her refuge, her home.

Millie changed out of her work clothes into pajamas and a robe and lay back on her bed, arms crossed behind her head, gazing out the window at the beautiful full moon. She loved Poplar Point and was content with her busy life in the small town. But tonight, her mind had unexpectedly opened itself to a new possibility.

Millie had never told anyone in the town anything about her background, not even Alice, and she intended to keep it that way. But overhearing those men and women talk tonight had lit a long–extinguished fire in Millie. The café was great. Indeed, she loved everything about it—its simplicity, the freshly made and locally sourced food, the customers. But unbeknownst to even her closest friends, Millie had money—a lot of money—sitting in a trust fund in New York. She had never felt the need to spend any of it, indeed had made a point of never touching it. But tonight, things had changed. She wanted to invest in the co–op. These farmers worked so hard, and for so little. She loved the idea of the shift in attitude toward marijuana benefitting people like them, rather than big corporations or, worse yet, criminal organizations. But no one must know—no one in Poplar Point or anywhere else. And there must be no way to trace the funds back to her.

Millie was absolutely certain that Grow Zone could flourish and that the farmers behind it were solid. While they might be able to scrape together enough to set up an operation held together with spit and glue, Millie wanted the town to shine. It needed a state–of–the–art growing facility that produced high quality flower with the least potential harm to the environment. She also knew that with some more money, they could spruce up the entire operation, helping to deflect the inevitable complaints that the sight of marijuana growing in nearby fields was somehow distasteful and bad for the town's reputation.

Millie resolved to call the bank in New York first thing in the morning. They would know how to set this up. As Millie reached over to turn off the bedside lamp, a wave of anxiety swept through her. There were reasons—serious reasons—why she never went near New York or the money. But now she had an opportunity to do something good. She had to be strong.

CHAPTER 15

ALICE

"Well, here we are. The first meeting of the Poplar Point Safe Access leadership team!" Bear was brimming with enthusiasm.

Alice looked around her living room. She couldn't believe it was only a week since they had met with Matt. And never in a million years could she have imagined this unlikely group of characters sitting here together.

Timmy sat on the couch blabbing on about something to his wife Willow who sat at his side. Alice noticed that Willow, owner of the Happy Hands Yoga and Massage Studio in town, seemed to be privately meditating while pretending to listen. Alice figured she'd had some practice at that. It was sometimes easy to dismiss Timmy. He wasn't the smartest or the best–looking, certainly not the most charismatic. But he was a good soul. Alice was impressed that he had taken time off several years ago to live in a Buddhist ashram and devote himself to yoga and meditation. He had returned with wife #3, the beautiful Willow, and had begun the weekly meditations at the church that Alice so enjoyed.

Alice next looked at Jed who was here tonight representing the Grow Zone Co–Op. Jed had taken a chair by the fireplace and looked the most comfortable of anyone in the group. He was probably happy to have a night out while Chrissie tended to Caleb.

And then there was Bill Smith, long–time owner of the town's hardware store. In many ways, Bill was an odd addition to the team. Alice suspected he had probably never even smelled marijuana. Although who knew—maybe Bill wasn't as strait–laced as Alice had always assumed. Still, she suspected he was as surprised as she was to find themselves comrades in arms.

Finally, there was Matt. Bear had introduced Matt to everyone and passed around various materials that Matt and their secret weapon Helen had put together.

As the group delved into a discussion of strategy, Alice noticed a shadow dart across the front lawn. Alert now, she began watching for movement out the window. There it was again! Someone was definitely hanging out around the front porch. Were there spies? That's impossible! Who even knew they were getting together tonight?

The more Alice thought about it, the more nervous she became. She knew the opposing forces were also organizing, and they would be only too interested in learning their strategy!

Alice was debating whether to say something to the group when a loud bang caused everyone to jump. After a rapid crisp knock, the front door swung open and in burst Alice's cantankerous next–door neighbor. Colonel Morehead, in his old Army jacket with his posture rigid and his crew-cut regulation length, was the scourge of the neighborhood kids. His "don't step on my grass" campaign had terrified every child in the town whose soccer ball had ever strayed onto his meticulously trimmed yard. Ha! Alice laughed to herself. Don't step on my grass. That's a good one!

"Alice!" he boomed. "I saw all the cars. What's going on here?" He looked around at the group suspiciously, his scrutiny landing on Bear and the Wentworths. "Ah ha! Is this something to do with marijuana?" He whirled back around to zero in on Alice. "You're not getting mixed up in this, are you, Alice? I know what goes on in this house, and I've respected your right to do as you please in your own home. But spreading this evil simply cannot be tolerated!"

Bill Smith stood and extended his hand. "Colonel, it's nice to see you."

Startled, the Colonel shook hands, confusion clouding his face. "Bill! I didn't see you there."

"Why, yes. And let me introduce Matt Jacobson who's down from Boston. Alice has been kind enough to let us gather here to talk about some business matters. Would you care to join us?"

"Oh, no, that's all right. I didn't mean to interrupt. I just wanted to make sure Alice was OK." Flustered, the Colonel backed toward the door, straightened, did an about–face and exited with as much dignity as he could muster.

"Well done, Bill!" exclaimed Jed, while everyone gave him a thumbs–up.

"That old busybody," muttered Alice.

"Yeah, well, when he figures out what we're really doing here, he is going to be pissed!" Bill noted. "I'm afraid that old busybody is just a hint of what's likely coming our way."

CHAPTER 16

HELEN

THAT SAME EVENING, HELEN SIGHED with relief as she heard the front door open. Rescued at last! Now on at least her hundredth game of gin rummy with Ben and Emma, Helen was eager to get back to work. She was surprised at how much she was enjoying spending time with her grandchildren, but an entire day with them home from school for a teachers' meeting was enough.

"Anybody home?"

"Mom! We're in here! Grandma taught us a new game!"

Ben and Emma both jumped up to give their mother a quick hug, then ran back to their seats and picked up their cards.

"I'll get dinner started while you all finish up." Kim folded her suit jacket neatly over the back of a chair and opened the refrigerator door.

"Well, actually, this has to be our last game. I've got some work to do, so I'm going to head up to my room for the evening.

"No, no! Can't we play some more?" both kids cried in unison.

"And don't you want some dinner, Mom?"

"Thanks, Kim, but I grabbed a bite earlier." Helen picked a card from the pile, discarded another, and, after declaring herself the winner, stood up. She tousled each child's hair and headed for the stairs. "Come give me a kiss before you go to bed!"

Helen could feel Kim's eyes on her as she headed for the stairs. She couldn't remember ever having played cards with Kim when she was little—or any game, for that matter. She and Jack had been so busy building their real estate business there never seemed enough time. Helen knew she had been missing in action for much of Kim's childhood and that Kim still resented it terribly.

As Helen climbed the stairs, her thoughts drifted to her own mother. Many a night while growing up, Helen had laid in bed and scoured her memory, searching for that moment when she first realized her mother didn't love her. Her mother had always meticulously cared for Helen's person, ironing her clothes, braiding her hair, driving her to playmates and ballet. But beyond that, she had been a tightly closed book, exuding no warmth. Helen had been relieved to get out of the house when she left for college.

Of course, Helen had had it easy compared to her father who had to face his wife's outright hostility every time he came home. Helen had never understood the source of all of her mother's anger and resentment, but she knew it ran deep.

As she reflected on her lack of a relationship with her mother, the realization of how perfectly she had duplicated the pattern with Kim bit deeply. No doubt some therapist would have a lot to say about that! Knowing how much she had been hurt by her own mother, how could she have turned around and so blithely ignored Kim's emotional needs? Fortunately, in a strange turn of events, Helen's mother had loved Kim to pieces from the moment she was born. Gram, as Kim called her, showered Kim with all the affection and warmth that had been bottled up for so long. Every year, Kim couldn't wait for summer to come so she could move in with Gram. Rather than feel jealous, Helen had been relieved that she could devote the summer to her work without feeling guilty. A sharp pain pierced Helen's heart as she thought of her own lonely childhood and her blind infliction of the same hurt on her daughter. Thank God Kim was a much better mother, even if she was awfully busy.

Helen settled into her chair and was soon immersed in marking up the first draft of the zoning amendment just released by the town's Planning and Zoning Committee in preparation for the upcoming Town Meeting vote. Several hours later, she was surprised by a knock on the bedroom door. She turned over the papers on her desk and closed her laptop as Kim entered the room.

"Mom, what are you so busy doing? Have you started working with Dad again?"

"Heavens no. That's not going to happen, Kim. It's just some other stuff."

"Real estate stuff?"

Helen thought hard. "Kind of."

"Are you thinking of selling real estate here?"

"No."

"Then what are you doing?"

"Uh, helping a friend." Helen could feel the heat creeping into her cheeks.

"Mom, are you seeing someone?"

"No! I mean, of course I see people—but I'm not *seeing* anyone!"

Kim noted Helen's flushed face and overly emphatic response. She smiled as she left the room. "Sure, Mom."

CHAPTER 17

BEAR

THREE WEEKS LATER, BEAR SAT at his usual table at Millie's, his large hand wrapped around a mug of steaming coffee. Bear loved Millie's, with its rough brick walls, old glass display counters, and checkered curtains.

Recently, though, the vibe at Millie's had changed. The entire town was in an uproar over the upcoming Town Meeting, with most of the local population passionately committed to one side or the other.

Poplar Point Safe Access and its opposition, Save Our Children, had been out in force. Poplar Point's usual quiet neighborhoods of old houses set back from the street with shade trees and colorful gardens were now battlefields of dueling yard signs. Even Millie's had experienced its share of raised voices, scowls, and fists banged on tables.

This morning, the café seemed to have temporarily settled. Still, Bear noted that most of the new patrons entering the door either came over to give him a slap on the back or studiously ignored him.

Millie, towel flung over her left shoulder, walked over to fill his mug. Shaking her head, she gave Bear a small smile. "I have to admit business has been booming, but honestly, I can't wait until this Town Meeting is over. It's like living in a war zone."

A young woman tentatively approached Millie from the kitchen, her apron reminiscent of a Jackson Pollock. "Sorry, Millie, but I can't find the nutmeg."

"Bear, have you met Rose yet?" Bear stared up into the softest brown eyes he had ever seen. Rose's thick dark hair was pulled back in a messy ponytail, and her face with its arched eyebrows, slightly prominent nose and full lips was speckled with flour. Rose absent–mindedly brushed back a stray strand of hair, adding yet another smudge to her cheek. "Hi, Bear, good to meet you." Rose smiled, and Bear was smitten.

"Likewise," said Bear, returning Rose's smile.

Millie looked at the two of them. "Well, I better get back to the counter," she said as she turned to leave. "Rose, can you take Bear's order?"

"Of course. Let me get you a menu, Bear."

Bear thought he detected a slight blush. "Don't bother. I'm pretty sure I've got it memorized."

Rose grinned. "OK, so what will it be?" She dug a notepad out of her pocket and withdrew a pencil that had been hiding in her hair.

"How about Millie's special? Eggs sunny–side up and rye toast."

"Got it."

As Rose walked away, Bear surprised himself by stopping her. "So where are you from, Rose?"

Rose stiffened, mumbling something about having been traveling.

"Well, welcome to Poplar Point. It's always nice to see a new face around here."

Rose turned back to face Bear. "Thank you! Honestly, everyone's been super welcoming. How long have you been here, Bear?"

"Forever—literally. Where are you staying?"

"I'm renting a room upstairs from Millie for the time being."

"Let's get together sometime. Not that there's all that much to see, but I can show you the local sights." *God, that sounded lame,* thought Bear. *Local sights? Why not my private etchings?*

"Great! I'd love that. I've gotta run, but here's my number." Rose scribbled her name and number on her order pad, tore out the sheet, and handed it to Bear.

"OK. I'll give you a call." Bear grinned. He couldn't believe he had actually stopped her and gotten her number.

Half an hour later, Bear headed out the door of Millie's, his step noticeably lighter. *Crap.* There was Marty, leaning against a lamppost, arms crossed, a Patriots hat pulled low over his face. Bear walked past, but Marty pushed off the lamppost and fell in step next to him.

Bear stopped abruptly and turned to face him. "Marty, I gave Jakie the money I owed you. I assume you got it?" Bear's face darkened as he remembered how upset his mom had been when he asked for the loan. He knew she suspected he had been dealing, and she wasn't pleased.

"Yeah, yeah, I got the money, but don't think that's the last of it. We know you're behind this pot legalization shit and that you and your mom have got ideas about setting yourselves up in business. Well, there's some people aren't gonna take to that. If you know what's good for you—and your ma—you'll rethink your plans."

"What the hell, Marty? This isn't just about my mom and me. The whole town is deciding, and we don't control the outcome. So leave my mom and me alone." Bear Kevin himself up to his full height and gave Marty a hard look. "And just so you know—next time you decide to mess with me, I'll be ready."

Marty shook his head. "You've gotta take this seriously, man. There's a lotta money at stake and there's people feeling the pressure. Opening pot shops around here is not good for their businesses."

"What people? What have you gotten yourself into?"

Marty veered off, crossed the street, and slid into a black Camaro with tinted windows. He tooted his horn as he sped away.

Bear had been half expecting this. Even so, the confrontation had left him shaken. Just who was Marty involved with now? Organized crime? And just how far would they be willing to go to try to block legit businesses? Bear thought about saying something to Patrick Graves, the town's police chief, but quickly reconsidered. He and Patrick hadn't been on the best of terms for years, and he couldn't imagine Patrick and his team of idiots taking on organized crime. Should he tell his mother? At least tell her to keep an eye out and lock her doors?

CHAPTER 18

ALICE

Several weeks later, Alice walked painfully into the house and collapsed in her chair, kicking her Dr. Scholls off. She propped her feet up on an old ottoman and looked across the room at Helen who was sitting primly in her usual chair waiting for her as promised.

"My feet are killing me!"

"Good grief, Alice! Your ankles look like watermelons!"

"Thanks, Helen. That's so nice of you to say. I doubt yours would look so perfect if you had done the amount of walking I have. Honestly, this vote better come soon or I'm not going to be around to learn the outcome."

"So, how's it going? It's so difficult waiting alone at home. Kim thinks I've lost my mind, always sitting in my room at my computer with the door closed. One night, she even asked if I was seeing someone!"

Alice gave Helen a skeptical look. "It's hard to tell, but I think things are going well. Bear and Bill and I have talked to all the businesses in town several times now, and we're definitely getting some positive feedback."

Alice watched as Helen's gaze traveled up and down Alice's prostrate form, taking in her baggy cotton pants and shapeless sweater. *Oh, no.... Here we go.*

"Do you think we should buy you some other clothes for your meetings, particularly the Town Meeting—something a tad more professional?"

"I don't know, Helen. Maybe we should stop by the thrift shop and pick you up some things so people don't think you got off on the wrong stop of the MBTA."

Helen blinked in astonishment. "I'm sorry, Alice. I knew I shouldn't say that." (*Whoa—did Helen just apologize?* thought Alice. *The world must be about to end!)* "It's just that I've been so stressed out. I can't sleep at night thinking of all the things we should be doing. I lie in bed for hours with my heart racing. And then sitting at the computer all day and night is killing me." Alice noticed Helen wincing as she tried to turn her head.

"Helen, I'm worried, too. A lot of people have a lot riding on this. But we can't let the pressure ruin our health. Uncontrolled stress is terrible for you, you know. Your neck, for example, looks awful. Have you tried meditating?"

"Me? Meditate? I'd rather shoot myself than sit cross–legged on the floor for 30 minutes humming or whispering or whatever it is you do."

"You don't have to sit cross–legged, Helen!" Realizing meditation was most likely a lost cause, Alice moved on quickly.

"I know! I have an appointment tomorrow at Willow's for a massage. You go instead of me."

Helen was horrified. "But I don't like massages!"

"You're kidding. Have you ever had one?"

"No. But I know I don't like them."

"Oh, don't be such an old fool, Helen. What is it you're so afraid of?"

"I am *not* afraid."

"Bullshit. I know afraid when I see it. Besides, this is exactly what you need for your neck. Think of it as physical therapy, but more comfortable. Come on, Helen—don't be such a chicken. Where's your spirit, girl? The appointment is at two, and I'm telling Willow to expect you. Your neck isn't going to get better on its own, so you might as well go."

"OK, OK. I'll give it a try."

Alice smiled. She knew she had pegged Helen right. Call her afraid, question her spirit, and Helen would always rise to the challenge. Besides, her neck really did look painful.

Both women gratefully turned toward the door as they heard the familiar sound of Bear's truck pulling into the driveway. Ah, saved by the Bear!

"Hey, Ma!" Bear burst into the house and stopped short, eyeing his mom stretched out in one chair and Helen perched on the edge of another. "You guys OK?"

"Fine, honey. Just bushed. Aren't you tired?"

"Yeah. But mostly I'm pumped. I think we're making progress. Your handouts have helped a lot, Helen." Bear headed toward the kitchen, pausing to give his mom a quick pat on the shoulder and to whisper in her ear, "And thanks, Ma. You're a real trooper."

Two minutes later, Bear was bustin' back through the living room, pointed toward the porch and his truck.

"Hey, slow down there, Bear! Where are you going in such a rush? Can't we talk for at least a minute?" Alice had hoped Bear might stay for supper.

But Bear already had one foot out the door. "Goin' out, Ma."

This is turning into a familiar pattern, thought Alice. "With anyone I know?"

Bear turned and gave her his best grin. "If things go the way I hope they will, you'll find out soon enough!" And then he was gone.

Alice looked at Helen, eyebrows raised.

An hour later, Alice stood at the kitchen sink, cleaning up her dinner dishes. She could picture her mother and her mother before her standing in this exact same spot, washing the evening dishes. Sure doesn't feel like the women in this family have made much progress, Alice thought to herself.

Alice's memory stretched back, recalling the day she was supposed to have left for college. Alice's inner voices had been screaming to her that day. *No! Don't go! This is not for you! This is not the right time!*

Most of the kids in her graduating class had anxiously awaited responses from their college applications, including Alice, but when the time for leaving finally came, she knew she couldn't go. Her grandmother had died only a year before, so now it was just her mom, her grandfather, and her. She could see her grandfather fading away since Nana had died, his step a little more faltering, his laugh a little more forced. How could she leave when her mom needed her?

And then there was Arlo who she had met over the summer at a music festival in a nearby town. Arlo had been a big, loveable man with an abundance of energy who saw joy all around him. For reasons Alice hadn't understood at the time, Arlo had chosen her, declaring her to be the one for him. Alice had been deeply surprised. But gradually Arlo had taught her to value herself, to have confidence in her instincts, and to believe in the rightness of her path.

Alice remembered marching down the stairs, through the living room, and across the screened porch to her mother and grandfather, who stood next to the loaded station wagon.

"I'm so sorry, but I've decided—I'm not going." Her mother and grandfather had frozen.

"But, Alice, this is the chance of a lifetime. This is your future!" Her mother had been near tears.

"No, Mom. I've made up my mind. My future is here—now. With you, and Grandpa—and maybe with Arlo."

Her mother had folded her in her arms, her forehead resting on Alice's shoulder.

"No, Alice. This is all my fault. I've depended on you way too much, held you too close, when I should have been preparing you to launch into the world. You have to go. You have to try."

Alice held her mother tightly. "Mom, this is not about you. This is about me. This is where I belong, where I want to be. Don't try to turn me into someone I'm not."

"Oh, Alice." Her mother began to cry.

"Mom, doors are opening all over for me. I can feel it. You just can't see them. I'm not afraid to go to college; I just don't want to. I'm one of the lucky ones. I already know who I am."

Her mother had straightened, wiping the tears from her eyes with her fingertips. "Alice, I have never made you do anything you didn't want to do. I will admit I have tried from time to time, but I have never succeeded. And here you are standing before me—a beautiful and strong young woman who knows her own mind. I'm so proud of you. But I am also sure that we can defer your acceptance in case you change your mind."

"Sure, Mom."

"So, is all the wailing finally over, and does this mean we start hauling all this junk back upstairs?" Grandfather had looked exasperated, but also secretly relieved. Alice was, after all, the life of this family.

CHAPTER 19

BEAR

Bear and Rose sat in a booth at The Good Earth, a cozy little café in the next town over where they had been several times before. Bear was feeling great. The Safe Access campaign was gaining steam every day, and on top of that, there was Rose.

Rose was beautiful, kind, and downright hilarious. Bear knew he was falling fast, but he wasn't so sure about Rose. She seemed happy to be with him, but so far at least, they were clearly just friends. Rose had shared very little about herself. She seemed surrounded by an as–yet impenetrable wall.

This evening, Rose had been uncharacteristically quiet. She seemed lost in thought now, staring out the window, her strong profile and long dark lashes reflecting the last golden rays of the setting sun.

Rose suddenly turned and looked Bear straight in the eyes. "Bear, there's something I've got to tell you.... I'm married."

Bear's heart sank, his jaw dropped. "What?"

"I'm married. It was a terrible mistake. I was living in Denver. It was a whirlwind romance, and he seemed so perfect. But it was a disaster." Tears welled in Rose's eyes. Bear reached across the table, taking both of her small hands in his large rough ones.

"I don't want to go into all the gory details, Bear; someday I will. What's important is I got away and drove to Boston, about as far away as I could get. I stayed in a women's shelter there for a while which is where

I met Millie. She asked me to come work for her in Poplar Point, and here I am. I've filed for a divorce, but it's gonna take some time."

"Oh, Rose. I am so sorry." Bear suddenly felt deflated. His shoulders sagged.

"I'm sorry it took me so long to tell you, Bear. No one knows but Millie, and I've just wanted to bury that part of my life. I've known that I have to tell you, but I didn't know what to say or what you would think." Rose grabbed her napkin as tears spilled down her face.

"You don't need to worry about me, Rose. It doesn't change anything between us. Hell, we've all made mistakes and you should be proud you had the guts to start over. This asshole just better hope we never run into each other. What's his name?"

"Tony."

"Hmm, Tony." Bear gently brushed a stray tear from Rose's cheek. "What about your family, Rose?"

"I don't have any family. My dad died in a car accident when I was ten, so my mom and I moved in with my grandparents. Not quite the happy situation that I gather you had with your mom and grandparents. My mom drank too much, and there was a lot of friction. They're all dead now. I'm sure part of the reason I married Tony so quickly is that I was excited to have a family again. His parents were so welcoming at first. It was only as time went by that I began to understand how much pressure Tony's dad put on him and the terrible effects it had on Tony."

"I hate to say it, but don't be too understanding. I get the sense Tony is not a nice guy."

"You're right about that. I just struggle with how I could have made such a terrible mistake."

"Anything else you want to tell me? You know I'm 100% here for you."

"Well, actually, there is."

Bear's heart clenched. Shit, he hadn't been expecting that. He looked at Rose apprehensively, trying not to show the anxiety that was rushing through his body.

"But this one might be kinda good."

"OK, spill it before you give me a heart attack."

Rose smiled. "Well, while I was in Denver, I worked a lot of jobs. For a while, one of them was waiting on customers at one of the bigger cannabis dispensaries."

Bear leaned his head back and ran his fingers through his thick hair. Recovering, he put his elbows on the table and leaned toward Rose. "Rose, that's awesome. You've been holding out on me."

They both laughed, relieved the conversation had moved on.

"Anything else, Rose?"

"Not right now."

"Thank God." They grabbed each other's hands, then turned their attention to the menus.

CHAPTER 20

HELEN

THE NEXT AFTERNOON HELEN SAT in the car in front of Willow's Happy Hands Yoga and Massage Studio, nervously fingering the strap to her purse. How had she let Alice talk her into this? Yes, she had been awfully uptight lately, and the stress of hiding her work on the marijuana store had been wearing on her. But a massage? Just the thought of taking her clothes off and lying on a table while a stranger touched her body was enough to send shards of tension down her shoulder blades. Helen slowly turned her head from side to side, checking to see if her turning radius had improved at all. Damn. She could barely get her chin halfway to her shoulder. She had to do something, and who knows—maybe this would help.

Helen resolutely got out of the car and walked up the steps into the studio. Well, this was a pleasant surprise. The walls were painted a beautiful delicate aqua and soft piano music played from a hidden speaker. Helen detected the faint scent of lavender, one of her favorites.

Just as she started to relax, Willow walked into the reception area followed by an older heavyset woman in a white coat. Good God, Willow was beautiful, a true flower child from the Sixties.

"Welcome, Helen. I hope we haven't kept you waiting." Willow's soft, lilting voice reminded Helen of Joni Mitchell. "This is Elise, one of my best masseuses. Elise will take you back to your room where you can get ready." Willow shook her head slightly, her long blond hair shimmering as it cascaded around her shoulders. "Alice told me this is your first massage. Just relax and enjoy your time with us. We're here to serve you. Anything you want or need, just tell Elise."

Helen followed Elise down a dimly lit hallway with several closed doors. Elise opened one of the doors and Helen hesitantly followed her in. Helen's first impression was that the room was small but tastefully decorated with the same soothing piano music playing in the background. Then her eyes focused on the table in the middle of the room. It reminded her of a hospital bed with its crisp white sheets. Or the table in an operating room! Helen was sure she wasn't going to like this.

"Helen." Helen jumped at the sound of Elise's voice. "I'm going to leave you now for a few minutes so you can undress. You'll find some hangers on the back of the door. When you're ready, slip under the sheet on the table on your stomach and relax."

Undress? Relax? "Take my clothes off? All of them?"

Elise smiled. "You certainly don't have to undress, but I can't do a massage through layers of clothing. If it makes you feel more comfortable, you can leave your underwear on."

"Well, that's a relief." Helen stared Elise down, determined to wipe that condescending smirk off her round doughy face.

"And if you want to use the ladies' room before we get started, it's right across the hall. I'll just step out now."

The door closed. Was it too late to make a run for it? Who says you have to stay if you don't want to? It's not like massages are mandatory or anything. Helen could picture it now—*Hey, lady. You just ran that red light! That'll be five massages by Tuesday!*

But Helen could imagine Alice's reaction if she wimped out. *Oh, Helen, it's such a shame you're so uptight. Honestly, a massage is so much better for you than a glass of Scotch!* And what would Willow think? Helen could see her now, laughing with her friends in town as she described Helen leaving the studio.

With a sigh of resignation, Helen undressed and neatly hung her clothes on the back of the door. She grabbed the white waffle robe lying on the bed and wrapped it around herself, knotting the tie securely. Slipping her feet into a pair of white paper slippers, she tentatively cracked the door open and looked down the hallway. Having assured herself the coast was clear, she closed the door behind her and headed into the bathroom across the hall.

A few minutes later, Helen emerged from the bathroom, ready to face her doom. She looked to the right. She looked to the left. Damn. Suddenly, she wasn't sure which door was hers. There were no markings on the doors, no letters or numbers to clue her in. Helen stared at the doors, reminded of a horrible old TV program. Is the prize behind Door #1, Door #2, or Door #3? Nobody ever got it right!

Palms starting to sweat, Helen padded across the hall and put her ear to Door #3. She couldn't hear a thing and there didn't seem to be any light spilling under the door. She padded down to Door #1. Shit, it was quiet, too. She was sure it wasn't Door #1. Helen thought hard and vaguely recalled going more or less straight across the hallway to the bathroom. Yes, that was it! It had to be Door #2!

Relief washing over her, Helen silently opened Door #2 and stepped into the room.

"Willow honey, I'm ready!" boomed a voice.

Helen took one look at the corpulent naked body lying on the table, a penis pointing straight as a flagpole at the ceiling, and screamed! Oh my God. It was Reverend Larson!

Helen ran as fast as she could to Door #3 with her damned paper slippers sliding all over the floor. She flung the door open, grabbed her purse and yanked her clothes off the hangers. Clothes grasped in one hand and shoes and purse in the other, she tore down the hallway, through the reception area and out the front door into the parking area.

"Helen! Helen! Where are you going??"

Helen didn't look back. She didn't want to talk to Willow now. Besides, she was quite sure Willow and the dear Reverend were going to feel more embarrassed by this episode than she was!

As she yanked her car door open, Helen noticed Bill Smith and Colonel Morehead standing on the sidewalk, mouths agape. Helen quickly checked that her robe was still in place, then threw her head back and smiled at the two men. "Good afternoon, gentlemen!"

Helen's tires spun in the gravel as she backed out of the parking space and sped off toward Alice's.

CHAPTER 21

ALICE

"ALICE!" HELEN'S VOICE REVERBERATED THROUGHOUT the house as she marched across the front porch and into the living room, still clutching her white waffle robe at her throat.

Alice clambered down the old stairs as quickly as she could, concerned by the note of hysteria in Helen's voice.

"Helen! What in God's name are you doing here in your bathrobe?" Alice was tempted to laugh, but one look at Helen's face told her that was not a good idea.

"Do you have anything to drink?"

"You mean like alcohol?"

"Of course I mean like alcohol! Get something for yourself, too—and not one of those funny cigarettes. We've got to talk!"

Alice returned momentarily with two glasses of sherry in her hands. Helen made a terrible face, but then emptied one of the small glasses in one gulp. Alice was worried. Had someone died? Was Helen sick?

Alice sat down and took a tiny sip of sherry. "OK, Helen. So what happened?"

As Helen described her experience at Willow's, Alice burst out laughing.

"Alice, this is not funny!"

Alice couldn't help herself. "Why, I'm surprised you could even see his penis over his fat stomach!"

"Alice, stop. This is the *last* time I am ever going to listen to you."

"*Me*? None of this is my fault. I can understand you might be upset."

"Might be upset? I am traumatized!" Helen's voice shook.

"Traumatized? Really? I mean—it's not like it's the first time you've seen a penis, Helen."

"Well, it's the first time I've seen Reverend Larson's!"

Alice tried to rein herself in and consider the situation from Helen's perspective. "Do you think he recognized you?"

"Judging from his expression and the haste with which he covered his privates, I would say probably yes. At the very least, Bill Smith and Colonel Morehead recognized me as I stormed out of the place in my bathrobe and stupid slippers."

"Oh, no, Helen." Alice started to laugh again. "That's pretty bad." Alice looked at Helen, who had unexpectedly gone quiet, eyebrows scrunched together and lines of intense concentration crisscrossing her forehead. Then Helen suddenly started laughing. A look of relief spread across her face. Alice watched her cautiously. Helen's abrupt mood changes did not always bode well.

"Alice, I just realized there may actually be a silver lining here. We have to make sure that the dear Reverend knows he was caught with his pants down!"

"Helen, no. I'm not sure what you're thinking, but we can't tell anyone about this."

"I'm not planning on telling anyone. We just need the Reverend to know that we know and to think that we *might* tell someone. I doubt his flock of Bible thumpers would be too pleased—nor would his wife!"

Alice winced at the thought of Faye's reaction if the story spread around town. Brendan might need a bodyguard, thought Alice, as she remembered the infamous Lorena Bobbitt.

Helen slapped her knees, stood up, and with one hand still pulling her robe tight, made for the door. "Alice, mark my word. I will never—I mean, *never* contemplate having a massage again. But this sure should take the wind out of the Reverend's sails, so to speak. I have to think about this!"

Alice's head was spinning as she leaned back in her chair and listened to the porch door slam behind Helen. What a mess. Picturing Helen bursting in on Brendan was hilarious, but the more Alice thought about it, the worse she felt.

Alice was disgusted by Brendan. Men were such pigs sometimes. She had always regarded him as something of a jerk, but deep down, she had envied his seemingly indomitable faith. What a joke.

And what the hell was Willow doing? Was this a one–time thing, or a regular service at Happy Hands? Happy Hands? Alice grimaced. Did Timmy know? Was he complicit? Even though she knew she was over–reacting, Alice felt terribly disappointed in Timmy and Willow. She had looked to them for spiritual leadership.

Alice knew she was overreacting. This was really no big deal. Everyone's just human after all. But she felt betrayed—and so alone.

Alice climbed the stairs to her room, put her yoga mat in the closet and dumped her gratitude journal in the trash.

CHAPTER 22

BEAR

FOLDING CHAIRS FILLED THE TOWN library's wood–paneled meeting room. Bear was surprised at the turn–out, and at the wide range of people. Not only were the chairs full, people were standing against the back wall and more were still waiting to enter. And this was only a Safe Access informational meeting!

Bear watched his mom as she walked in with Rose. *Uh oh. Wonder what they've been talking about?* Alice slowly worked her way to the front of the room to the seat he and Millie had saved for her.

Bear walked to the long tables in the hall where volunteers were taking names and contact information from folks interested in helping. Bear couldn't believe the number of people who had signed up. After giving the crowd a few more minutes to settle, he moved to the small table at the front. Boy, was he glad to see Matt and Jed and Bill! Heart pounding in his chest, his voice cracked as he called the meeting to order.

"Welcome everybody. Thank you all for comin' out tonight. We all know we've got an important vote comin' up next week at the Town Meeting. We've got some folks here who want to share with you why they think it would be a huge mistake to put a ban on the sale of marijuana in Poplar Point Township. To be clear, plenty of marijuana is sold and smoked in Poplar Point and has been for years. We're not talking about turning every man, woman, and child in the town into a dope–smoking deadhead."

"Aw, why not, Bear?" someone shouted from the back of the room. A few appreciative chuckles followed.

Bear ignored the interruption. "In all seriousness, by legalizing and regulating the sale of marijuana, we can make things safer for everyone. Plus, as you'll hear, there is money in this for the town—much–needed money."

"Now you're talkin', Bear!" another voice boomed out. The increasingly comfortable crowd clapped enthusiastically.

Bear introduced Matt, who gave a quick run–down of the business concept and projected financial benefits for the town. And then, as planned, townspeople stepped forward to share their views and ask their questions.

First up was Jed, who was holding a squirming child in his arms. "For any of you who don't know me, I'm Jed Dawson and this is my wife Chrissie and my little trouble–maker Caleb. We own the old Millstone Farm a couple miles outside of town. We and our friends here are all farmers and you may recognize us from the vegetable co–op we run in the summer."

Everyone in the audience nodded appreciatively.

"Chrissie and I came here with a dream of living sustainably off the land. And, well, it's been tough. We work hard, real hard, but the cash flow simply isn't there. We need a cash crop we can sell locally if we're going to keep our dream alive."

"But what about our summer vegetables, or are you planning on us getting our greens another way?" a voice called out.

Everyone laughed. Chrissie stuck her head around Jed. "No need to worry, Pete. You'll still get your veggies."

Next up was Bill, sporting his usual crew–cut, khakis and collared shirt with Poplar Point Hardware printed on the pocket. "Now I'm not here to advocate anyone smoke marijuana or to judge anyone who does or doesn't." ("Well, that's a relief, Bill!" someone in the audience shouted.) "But I am here to tell you I absolutely believe it would be a mistake for the town to ban the legal sale of cannabis in Poplar Point. Provided the proper safeguards and regulations are put in place and enforced, we can't afford to forego this opportunity."

Soon others were joining the conversation, asking questions and offering their views. Just as Bear started to relax, the door burst open and in marched Colonel Morehead. Arm raised as though he were leading a charge, the Colonel was followed by a group of townspeople, all waving small American flags and wearing "Save Our Children!" tee–shirts. The Colonel stopped, glared at Alice, then pointed his finger at Bear: "I knew you were up to no good!"

CHAPTER 23

ALICE

ALICE STARED AT THE COLONEL and shook her head. She was surprised to see him, although, on reflection, she shouldn't have been. They had been uncomfortable neighbors ever since the Colonel had moved to his wife's family's old homestead in Poplar Point after he retired from the Army about ten years ago. Having grown up in a military family as had his father before him, the transition to a civilian life had been difficult for the Colonel, who often struck Alice as a parody of a Patton-esque General who had somehow misplaced his army. After the death of his wife a few years back, things had only gotten worse. The Colonel had assumed the role of neighborhood policeman, setting out orange cones every afternoon when school let out to ensure no parent parked illegally, and chasing down any poor soul who committed one of the cardinal sins of littering or failing to pick up after the family dog. He and Alice had come to a truce of sorts. After all, she was just a poor, misguided woman who hadn't had a properly upstanding, right-minded man to guide her. Bear, on the other hand, was regarded by the Colonel as a total abomination. The Colonel looked positively gleeful as he led a group of the Save Our Children converts into the library with the clear intent of disrupting Bear's meeting.

As people stood, a couple of folding chairs collapsed and crashed to the floor. Insults flew as tempers flared. Alice could hear Bear yelling, "People, everybody, quiet down! Take your seats!" But no one was listening.

After weeks of feeling like she had to defend herself to half the community, Alice was fed up. She stood and worked her way to the speakers' table, put two fingers in her mouth, and blew an ear–splitting whistle. Miraculously, the room quieted.

"Everybody needs to take a deep breath. This is not the Poplar Point I know. This is not how we behave. We have an absolute right to gather together and to talk—without interruption."

Alice returned to her seat, totally surprised that she had stood and spoken. She was even more surprised at the smattering of applause.

Colonel Morehead turned on Alice. "Well, meeting to discuss bringing drugs to our town is not exactly the Poplar Point I know, either. We agree you have the right to talk. We just want to make sure you understand that most of the town is united against you, and this will never happen!"

"You got that one wrong, brother!" someone in the audience called out.

The Colonel shook his head disparagingly as he and his band of brothers—and sisters—exited, still waving their flags and staring with cold, uncompromising eyes at the Safe Access crowd.

Still talking among themselves, everyone eventually sat back down. Bear soon closed the meeting, thanking everyone for coming and for all the offers of help. As Alice moved with the crowd into the hall and to the open library door, she spotted Reverend Larson across the parking lot, arms crossed, a superior smirk on his face. His eyes were locked on Bear. His deep voice echoed across the space. "You know this isn't right, don't you, Bear? We can't let you corrupt our town and kill our children."

Alice was appalled. She started to shout back, but caught herself. Best to ignore him—for now. As she turned back toward Bear, she saw he was frowning, fixated on something at the other end of the parking lot. She followed his gaze and spotted Marty Doyle leaning against a shiny black Camaro. Two men she didn't recognize were standing next to him. Bear took Alice's arm and shepherded her back into the library. Hmm. Alice looked at Bear inquiringly.

CHAPTER 24

ALICE

LATER THAT EVENING, ALICE LEANED back in her chair, savoring the moment. Millie had been so thoughtful, reopening the café so the Safe Access team could regroup and debrief after what had been an unexpectedly eventful evening.

Alice gazed around the candle–lit table, soaking in each person's essence and sending out vibes of gratefulness for their goodness and friendship.

"Well, we sure had a nice–sized crowd tonight. Frankly, I was surprised." Bill was obviously enjoying himself. Who knew?

"What you're really trying to say, Bill, is you were surprised to see so many of your clean–cut, church–going friends at the meeting."

"Well, you've got a point there, Bear."

"Oh, Bill, they're just following your lead, wanting to be cool like you!" Chrissie smiled as she carefully rearranged now sleeping Caleb in her arms. They all laughed, including Bill.

"It kills me to think of all those flag–wavers home now smoking their cigarettes and drinking their cocktails. Don't they understand the harm *that* causes?" Everyone around the table looked at Timmy and nodded. "But don't you worry—Bear and I have a trick or two up our sleeves that ought to get everyone's attention." Timmy winked at Bear.

Alice wasn't sure what she thought of Timmy and Willow these days, but they certainly spent a lot of time in la–la land, even by Alice's standards.

"Well, I'm not sure you need any tricks," said Millie, standing by the table with an empty pitcher in her hand. "Bear, you did an amazing job tonight organizing everything, and tons of people signed up to help. And Alice, you brought some sanity to an absolutely insane situation. Well done!" Millie gave her a wink. "I think we should feel encouraged."

Bear cleared his throat.

"Thanks, Millie. And thanks to you all. This has been a team effort all the way. I'm feeling hopeful all our hard work is paying off. But there's something I have to tell you."

The group quieted and turned toward Bear. Alice felt a twinge of unease; it wasn't like him to make surprise announcements. Bear took a deep breath.

"Do any of you know Marty Doyle?"

"Sure do," said Jed, "and he's bad news." Chrissie nodded her head.

"Well, Marty works now with a nasty group of drug dealers based in Fall River, and he and his friends have cornered the market around here for major drug sales. Not just marijuana, but other stuff, too. He and his friends seem to have decided that making the sale of marijuana legal here will be bad for business. And as most of you know, Fall River doesn't offer a lot of other economic opportunities for guys like Marty. He has, well, he's kinda made some threats."

Alice's heart clenched. "What threats?" she asked, her voice wavering slightly.

"Nothin' specific. Just that I better not go through with this, or I'll be sorry. Tonight, he and a couple of other tough–looking guys were standing in the parking lot after the meeting. I'm not worried, but I thought it only fair to tell you all."

"I'm not so sure you shouldn't be worried, son." Bill frowned. "I would agree with you if it were *only* Marty, but I'd say it all depends on who he's hooked up with. What do you know about his partners, Bear?"

"Not much," said Bear, looking down at the table. "I haven't had any direct dealings with them, but it's clear Marty takes them seriously. He seemed kinda scared the last time I talked with him, and I'm assuming he's gotten himself in deep with one of the Fall River gangs."

Alice saw a look pass between Chrissie and Jed. "Ahem." Jed raised his hand. "We've gotten some threats, too. Mostly notes left on the barn door." Alice noticed how Jed's arm tightened around Caleb protectively.

"Us, too," said Timmy, reaching for Willow's hand. "Nothing specific. Just that we better back off."

Alice was close to tears.

"Well, I'll be damned," said Bill. "Are Alice and Millie and I the only ones here they haven't threatened?"

"Actually, Marty did kinda mention you, Ma." Bear glanced at Alice sheepishly.

Alice felt like she had been slapped on the side of the head. It had never even occurred to her that some people stood to lose something if the amendment passed.

Bill frowned. "Has anyone talked to the police?" Five pairs of eyes rolled. "I know, I know. They aren't exactly the sharpest tools in the box."

"It's worse than that, Bill," said Bear. "Patrick Graves' commitment to protecting the town from serious crime has primarily consisted of hassling anyone in the town he suspects of using marijuana."

"Well," said Bill, "I'm going to talk to Patrick anyway, so he knows to keep an eye out. That's why we have a police force after all. And we all need to let each other know if we see or hear anything else."

Well, that sure put a damper on an otherwise awesome evening, thought Alice. *Now I suppose I will have to tell Helen. Man, she's gonna love this. Threats from drug dealers. Might be more than she bargained for.*

With that, the group broke up, thanked Millie, and moved en masse out the door. The women hugged and the men shook hands. Alice sensed that the group was more tightly bound together than ever as they parted for the night. It seemed the stakes had been raised.

CHAPTER 25

ALICE

After a sleepless night, Alice called Helen the next morning to ask if she could stop by. Helen immediately said yes. Kim, Kevin and the kids were all off to work and school, so it was only Helen and their sad sack of a dog, Walter, at home.

Alice arrived in record time to find Helen finishing up the dishes, a pot of coffee and mugs already on the table.

"Helen, something came up last night I thought you should know about. Honestly, I had no idea. I don't know what I would have done if I had, but never in a million years would I have expected this. I feel so stupid. And so bad for Bear and the others."

"Alice, would you sit down and slow down? I don't have a clue what you're talking about."

Alice sat in a chair at the polished kitchen table, continuing to talk after barely taking a breath.

"Did you ever run across a guy named Marty Doyle or his parents? Marty's about the same age as Bear and Kim. He's a real troublemaker, has been since he was young. His parents were alcoholics. Lived out by the dump in a falling down house, and they plain ignored that boy. By the time he got to high school, Marty was mean as a great white. In all sorts of trouble."

Helen sighed and put her head in her hands. "Alice," she said in a strained voice, "what are you talking about? What has any of this got to do with me? Can you just get to the point?!"

"Well, you see, Marty's been dealing drugs around here for years. Half the people in town have bought from him at one time or another. But then he moved on to bigger stuff, too—meth, fentanyl, some even say heroin. Bear says he runs with a pretty rough crew from Fall River."

"So?" Helen tapped her perfectly manicured nails on the table, a clear sign her patience was running thin.

"So he's threatened Bear. And Jed and Chrissie, and Timmy and Willow. And who knows who else. Said they better back off from this store idea or there would be trouble. I just found this out last night." Alice started to tear up. "I'm so sorry, Helen. The thought that this hare–brained idea of ours might get someone hurt is *really* upsetting. I would understand if you wanted out." Alice blew her nose and looked across the table at Helen, fully expecting to see Helen as shaken as she was.

Helen stared at Alice for a minute, then got out of her chair and calmly walked upstairs. Alice could hear her rummaging around a bit. Then she came back into the kitchen and placed something on the table with a loud thunk.

Alice stared at it wordlessly. A gun! Alice had been around hunting all her life and had seen plenty of rifles and shotguns. But this was a nice, neat little handgun with a pink grip.

"What the hell, Helen!"

"No two–bit punk is going to mess with me and interfere with my perfectly legal right to advocate for something the state legislature has already blessed. From now on, this baby goes everywhere with me, and I suggest you get one, too."

"But, Helen, could you actually shoot someone?"

"If I had to, hell yes! I wouldn't want to, but this is America and people have to stand up for their rights. If you and Bear and I want to open a marijuana store and the state and town say it's all right, then that's exactly what we're going to do. No two–bit hood is going to stop us!"

Alice looked at Helen in disbelief. Who was this woman? Where was Miss Namby–pamby, oh boo hoo I lost my man, and damn I broke my fingernail?

Alice sure as hell wasn't getting a gun, but she regarded Helen with new respect and more than a little consternation. Too bad Marty and his pals didn't know Helen was part of the group. Why, they could sic Helen on them!

Alice sat up straighter, wiped her eyes, and took a sip of coffee. "Why, Helen, I'm not sure this is at all helpful, but I quite admire you. Now would you get that damn gun off the table?"

CHAPTER 26

ALICE: FIRST TOWN MEETING

THINGS SEEMED TO HAVE SETTLED down somewhat over the past week. Neighbors were talking to neighbors again, and nearly everyone was abiding by an unspoken agreement to take a break from the petitions, handouts, and signs. But divisions in the town still ran deep, and everyone knew tonight's Town Meeting was an important one.

By 7:45, the parking lot was past full, all chairs had been taken, and a quorum had long since been reached. Alice stared at the room in amazement. Never had she seen so many people at a Town Meeting! And they weren't even voting tonight—just sharing their views.

Alice and Bear sat nervously in the front row, Alice wringing her hands while Bear's knee bounced up and down like a high–speed jackhammer. Alice reached up to touch her hair, reassuring herself that her long, wavy gray mane was at least somewhat under control. She unconsciously patted her subtly tie–dyed purple dress, hoping she looked respectable.

Alice glanced at Bear next to her, noting that he, too, had cleaned up. Her heart squeezed as a wave of affection washed over her. It had meant a lot to her these past few weeks watching him work so hard to prepare for this meeting. It was as though a new Bear had been born.

Alice had always known people liked Bear. He was unassuming, kind, and generous. Even so, the depth of Bear's connection to the town's people and the warmth with which most of them greeted him had been gratifying. Bear could talk to anyone—old, young, rich, poor—and seem to understand where they were coming from. Helen's talking points had provided Bear with ready facts and figures, but Bear had made the pitch his own, knowing intuitively how to fine–tune it depending on his audience.

Alice watched the people crowding into the Town Meeting, some of them leaning against the walls. This had to be a record turn–out! She found herself silently praying. Not that she believed in the power of prayer. But so much depended on these people.

CHAPTER 27

BEAR: FIRST TOWN MEETING

Bear's palms were slick, his knees shaky. He glanced nervously over his shoulder. Holy shit! The room was full, with people standing in the back, including, to his surprise, Helen, who had sworn she was going to stay home.

Bear was happy so many of their supporters and friends had come, and appreciated their encouraging nods and smiles. But the Reverend's and Colonel's troops were out in full force, too, having made quite the grand entrance. It felt a bit like being at a wedding, with the bride's family sitting on one side and the groom's on the other. A wedding, that is, where the two sides hated each other and were bitterly opposed to the impending marriage.

Bear turned back toward the front as the five members of the Board of Selectmen filed in to take their seats. As always, Bear's breath caught as Kim walked in. She was dressed in her usual dark, no–nonsense business suit with her best school principal look on her face. But Bear had never forgotten the beautiful, passionate woman inside.

His mind wandered for a minute, savoring the memory of their short–lived secret romance one summer in high school. Bear was confident that they had had a deep connection and that Kim had truly cared about him. He had been crushed when Kim broke off the relationship before school restarted, begging Bear not to tell anyone about their time together. He never had, although he had been doubly hurt by Kim's insistence on secrecy. Was she embarrassed by him? Or was it all about the long–standing feud between their grandmothers? Or just that Kim had known, even then, that they had no long–term future together. No matter, he always remembered what he considered to be the "real Kim."

Bear's mind snapped back like a taut rubber band. He checked the crowd once again, ensuring that all the leaders of Poplar Point Safe Access were there, and that Marty and his goons were nowhere in sight. So far, so good.

Bear breathed a sigh of relief as Matt walked in the door. Matt had been a real godsend. He was a hard–headed entrepreneur, but no matter the stress, he always projected an air of calm and assurance. He had been tremendously helpful not only to the Safe Access team but also to the farmers who were struggling to pull together their Green Zone Co–Op. Helen had sure been on the right track this time! After Helen had whispered a suggestion in Bear's ear, the team had decided to let Matt be their opener since he could describe first–hand the experiences of other towns that had opted to permit cannabis sales.

Bear saw Matt glance at Helen with a touch of surprise and then search the crowd for Alice. Bear loved watching Matt handle the two women, although he occasionally found his attentiveness a bit overdone. Helen and Alice had driven everyone crazy as they argued like an old married couple about the most insignificant details. But Matt, the ultimate diplomat, seemed attuned to the deeper differences and misunderstandings that underlay their disagreements. As a result, he was able to resolve almost every issue, leaving both women feeling they had reached the right decision. A perfect example had been their fight over the Safe Access message. Should they be emphasizing the medical benefits, particularly of the CBD products, as Helen wanted, or the general well–being benefits of the more traditional THC products preferred by Alice? Matt had managed to persuade them that the medical and well–being benefits of marijuana were complementary, rather than in conflict. Of course, Helen and Alice deserved some credit, too, mused Bear. In some ways, they were a lot more alike than either of them cared to admit.

CHAPTER 28

HELEN:
FIRST TOWN MEETING

Helen leaned against the back wall, trying to be as inconspicuous as possible. She hadn't planned on coming, but at the last minute she couldn't bear to stay away. She knew Kim had already seen her, but Kim hadn't seemed particularly surprised; lots of people came to Town Meetings.

Helen spotted Matt as he came in the door. Thank goodness he had agreed to be the primary speaker for their side. Bear and Alice had been a little unsure about having an "outsider," but she suspected they were also more than a little relieved. Really, their chances would *not* be enhanced by having an unemployed man who lived in a trailer and his hippie mother representing them.

Helen felt a twinge of guilt at her own pettiness; Alice and Bear had worked hard, and they did have a lot of friends. Still, this *was* business.

Helen studied the crowd. If she had to guess, she would say their side had the better turn–out. Just as she began to feel confident, more of the Reverend's flock arrived, some of them singing "We Shall Overcome" as they entered the hall. *What idiots. Did they think God spent his time figuring which towns should sell marijuana? I mean, he created the stuff, didn't he?*

Kim rose and stepped to the microphone. "Ladies and gentlemen, this Town Meeting is called to order. Jeremy, would you read the minutes from the last meeting?"

"I move the reading of the minutes be waived."

"Seconded."

"All in favor? So ordered."

Kim briskly continued: "As you know, cannabis is now legal in the state, and each township has the right to decide whether to allow the sale of recreational marijuana within its borders. A group, Poplar Point Safe Access, has asked the Board and the Planning and Zoning Committee to amend the town's zoning laws to permit the licensing of one marijuana store. The Board, the Planning and Zoning Committee, and the Finance Committee have all announced their opposition to such an amendment. However, because the Town Meeting has the final say and the community seems deeply divided, the Planning Committee and we have drafted a detailed zoning amendment that spells out the many regulatory requirements a store would have to comply with before it could sell recreational marijuana."

Kim began to run through a long list of regulations. Helen couldn't suppress a small smile. Kim was bossy and could be a pain in the ass, but Helen was incredibly proud of her.

Helen caught Matt looking at her. A slight tip of his head and upturn at the corner of his lips acknowledged her presence. Helen felt her cheeks redden. She returned the nod and turned away.

Finally, it was time for the speakers. As planned, Matt, Bear, Jed and Bill each rose and gave their short, but well–rehearsed and carefully reasoned presentations. Helen was surprised by the number of other pro–amendment residents who made comments: a young local doctor, the town pharmacist, long–time business owners, and a few parents. Each of them emphasized the advantages of regulating and controlling a substance that had already made a home in their community.

The anti–amendment speakers started off equally reasoned and dispassionate. They voiced their concerns about increased access to drugs, listed all the health risks, and talked about the research showing the harmful impact on brain development in the young.

The crowd tensed when Mary Jenkins raised her hand and rose to speak. She grasped a handkerchief in one hand and began in a quivering voice. "As most of you know, our 24–year–old son Ben died two months ago from an opioid overdose. I don't think our family will ever get over this."

Mary looked down, then raised her head to look around the room. "We had known since he was in high school that Ben and his friends occasionally smoked marijuana. We did everything we could to convince him not to. Then a couple of years ago, Ben had a motorcycle accident and injured his leg. His doctor prescribed OxyContin for the pain and, well, you all know the rest of the story.

"I can't say marijuana caused Ben's death or even for sure that it's a 'gateway drug' like some people say. But I do ask myself every day, if Jim and I had been stricter, if Ben had never smoked marijuana, would his story have ended differently? Drugs are terrible, and it makes no difference if they are legal or illegal except that they are easier to get if they are legal." Mary sat down amid a smattering of sympathetic applause. Her husband put his arm around her and Kevin her close.

Many in the audience had tears in their eyes. Helen wiped at her own, imagining for a moment the searing pain of losing a child. Helen was momentarily shaken. Was the other side right? Were they involving themselves in something that was going to be bad for the town no matter how much money it brought in?

Helen thought back to all the reading she had done and the many inconclusive and conflicting studies about the possibility of a connection between marijuana use and opioid deaths. The truth was marijuana, like alcohol and even tobacco, affected different people differently. And so far, the research suggested marijuana was the least dangerous of the three.

Helen started to worry the crowd might be persuaded that the lives of Poplar Point's youth truly did turn on the outcome of this vote. But then Reverend Larson rose to his feet. Helen hadn't seen him since her ill–fated trip to Happy Hands. A small groan escaped her lips.

Hands held high, voice booming, the Reverend launched into a hell–and–brimstone sermon. "How can God–fearing, righteous citizens consider legalizing the sale of drugs in our town, all in the name of making a buck? How can we face our children, knowing they see our hypocrisy?

That we value business over our community's health and safety? Does regulating something we all know in our hearts to be wrong miraculously make it right?"

As the Reverend wound up, the temperature in the hall rose. Whispered words of approval competed with snickers and snide comments. Then the Reverend crossed the line.

"We all know that marijuana rots your brain and destroys your motivation. Marijuana affects attention, memory, and the ability to think clearly for days or even weeks after use. Recent studies have found that those who smoke weed don't do as well in school, are less likely to complete college, and tend to be less successful." The Reverend stared straight at Bear and continued. "We've got living proof of that right here in this room."

There was a small gasp in the room. Everyone knew the Reverend was referring to Bear.

Something snapped inside Helen. Pushing off the wall, she pulled herself to her full height and, without thinking, shouted out: "That's ridiculous! You don't have any idea what you're talking about! Have you read the statistics? Weed, or whatever you want to call it, is far less dangerous than alcohol—or tobacco—or guns!"

"Mom!" Kim's voice reverberated in the hall. Helen took in the look of shock and disbelief on Kim's face. But it was too late now. Helen threw her shoulders back and announced to the crowd: "I've never smoked marijuana, nor do I have any plans to do so. But if adults want to, they should be able to do so safely and without fear of the police or the judgment of their neighbors." Helen turned and looked squarely at the Reverend. "As Jesus said, let he that is without sin among us cast the first stone!"

Reverend Larson stared at Helen, then suddenly seemed to recognize her. He blanched and abruptly sat down.

At that moment, the door to the hall blew open and in stepped Timmy from the Senior Center across the street. No, wait—not just Timmy but an entire brigade of elderly residents, some with canes, some with walkers and a couple in wheelchairs. They quietly spread down the aisles of the room, blocking all ingress and egress.

Roy Collins, the eldest resident of Poplar Point, spoke clearly in a firm voice: "We are here to lend our support to Poplar Point Safe Access and to ask this town to do the right thing and approve the amendment." It took a minute for the audience to take in the signs carried by the brigade: "Safer than alcohol." "Safer than smoking." "Safer than my meds. Have you read the side effects?" "Life is too short not to enjoy it." "Without pot, weed be gone!"

At first a few people cheered. Then all hell broke loose. One side of the crowd began clapping, hooting and generally congratulating the Live Strong brigade, while the Save Our Children crowd accused Timmy and Safe Access of duping these old people into staging an outrageous stunt. Kim slumped in her seat, while her vice chair tried to call the meeting to order.

"Ladies and gentlemen. Let me have your attention for just a minute. This seems like a good time to break. Are there any questions about the details of the proposed zoning amendment? No? Well then, I think we will call it a day—or night. Thank you to everyone who shared their views. We all certainly have a lot to think about. The Town Meeting will reconvene next Wednesday, same place, same time. All town residents over the age of 18 are eligible to vote."

Almost no one was listening, the room in sheer pandemonium. The Board members closed their notebooks and made a hasty exit out the back. As everyone else rose and rustled on jackets and coats, lively discussions, some of them heated, reverberated around the room. The Live Strong brigade made its stately way out of the hall and then, with unenthusiastic police escort, safely back across the street.

Helen pushed her way through the crowd, searching for Kim, but she was nowhere to be seen. How was she going to explain to Kim that she had been working on this for weeks without telling her?

As she worked her way through the crowd, a number of people who Helen had barely seen since high school said hello, some even going so far as to pat her on the back or shake her hand. Helen wasn't sure if she was pleased or horrified. Well, for better or worse, she was certainly out of the closet now.

CHAPTER 29

KIM

HEAD DOWN, KIM EXITED THE rear of the Town Hall and headed to her car. Without so much as a nod to anyone, she climbed in and fastened her seatbelt. But where was she going? Home to tell Kevin what had happened? To tell her children that the grandmother they had come to love was now the town champion of marijuana?

Kim managed to wend her way out of the parking lot before the traffic got snarled. She sped toward the house. After pulling into the driveway, Kim smoothed her hands over her suit and carefully composed her face, telling herself to take a deep breath. This wasn't the end of the world. Lots of parents and children disagreed about things.

But Kim was totally shocked—and hurt. Why was her mother, of all people, speaking up for the Safe Access side? Was this what her mother had been secretly working on up in her room all this time? She knew about Kim's position as chair of the Board and principal of the high school; she knew about the public stance Kim and the rest of the Board had taken. Didn't she care that Kim now looked like a fool? And how could her mother think it was OK to show up at her house after all this time anyway? Things were already at the breaking point with Kevin and having her "little miss perfect" mother around didn't make it any easier. Didn't her mother get it?

Having now worked herself into a rage, Kim stomped up the steps and into the front hallway. Toys and clothes were scattered everywhere, with nary a soul in sight. "Kevin? Kids? Where are you?"

Two small voices answered from upstairs. "We're watching TV, Mom."

Kim marched up the stairs. She had told Kevin to put the kids to bed. It was a school night after all. How irresponsible could he be?

Kim reached the TV room and was astounded to see Shelley, the teenager from down the street, sitting with her two children.

Shelley looked up and smiled. "Hi, Mrs. West."

"Wh–h–haaat are you doing here? Where's Kevin?"

"I don't know. He called and asked if I could babysit for a while. He said he would be home before you got home." Shelley shifted uncomfortably.

"Emma, Ben!" Kim stood in front of the television to get their attention. "Do *you* know where your dad is?"

"Nope." They each glanced her way but quickly returned their full attention to their TV program.

Just then, Kim heard the front door open. She ran down the stairs, almost tripping over a shoe left on one of the steps. *These damn heels!*

"Kevin, what the heck?" Kim was furious but mindful of the children upstairs. "Where have you been?"

As Kevin moved toward her and began to open his mouth to speak, she smelled her answer. The scent of stale beer overwhelmed her, mixed with the slightest hint of perfume. Kim took in Kevin's rumpled hair and the pale lipstick smear on his chin. She stared at Kevin in disbelief. She had known things were bad, and deep down she had even suspected he was cheating on her. But she had chosen to look the other way, to assume that her suspicions were unfounded. To have confronted Kevin would have risked confirming the worst and might have forced her to admit that her marriage was a failure. Now what choice did she have when he had chosen to be so blatant about it, sneaking out when he was supposed to be watching the kids and she was at a Town Meeting of all things?

"That's it, Kevin. We're done. How could I have been so stupid?"

"You're overreacting. There's nothing wrong with me going out for a bit. The kids are fine, they love having Shelley babysit them, and you feel free to go out whenever you choose. I heard things got a little out of hand at the meeting tonight. Is that what's got you so bent out of shape?"

"You're right, Kevin. The meeting was a disaster. But that's not the problem. *You're* the problem. *We're* the problem. *Our marriage* is the problem. I know you've been seeing someone else."

Kevin made no effort to stop her as she grabbed her purse and keys off the side table and ran down the steps to the Tahoe. Slamming the heavy car door behind her, she punched the ignition button, turned on the lights and backed the behemoth out of the driveway. Two blocks later, she pulled over, put the car in Park, and burst into tears. She slammed her hands against the steering wheel until they hurt.

What a terrible night. Everything was going wrong—had been going wrong for some time now. Now what was she going to do? Where was she going to go?

Kim slumped in her gigantic heated leather seat and cried some more. She needed someone to talk to, to console her and tell her everything would be all right. She had friends, but no one she could share this with; they all knew her through her position at school. And talking to her parents had never been an option! If only Gram were still alive. She would know what to do.

Finally, she put the car in Drive again and eased out into the road, eyes focused straight ahead. She knew where she was going. She needed someone she could trust, someone who knew her and would listen to her for a change.

As she knocked on the door of Bear's brightly lit trailer, she yelled out. "Anybody got a drink around here?"

CHAPTER 30

ALICE

Alice pulled into her driveway, feeling totally drained. Did Brendan understand how much pain he was causing by painting her and other supporters of legal sales as immoral money–grubbers who cared nothing for the well–being of the town? And the look on Bear's face when Brendan had gone after him! It had nearly broken Alice's heart. Was this all worth it? Alice had not fully appreciated the size of the hornets' nest they were poking when they launched their little venture.

Alice turned off the lights and opened the door, dragging herself out of the car. She had to stop sitting in those damned folding chairs.

As Alice straightened, she caught sight of a shrouded figure standing in the deep darkness cast by the old elm in the side yard. Alice's heart caught in her throat. Should she jump back in the car, or try to make it to the front door? Damn, why hadn't she asked Bear to follow her home?

"Alice," a voice called to her softly.

"Faye," Alice answered in surprise. "Is that you? What are you doing here?"

"Waiting for you."

A chill ran down Alice's back. *Waiting for her? What the hell for*? Alice wasn't sure what was up with Faye, but she had been making her uncomfortable recently. Alice turned and closed the car door, then walked to the edge of the driveway as Faye crossed the lawn toward her. "Faye, do you want to come in?"

"Good God, no. Brendan or one of his followers might see me. Consorting with the enemy? My, my. That wouldn't do."

"Well, then, what can I do for you?"

"There's nothing you can do for me. I'm a goner. Past my prime. Just waiting for the exit sign to light up. No, the question is, what can I do for you?"

Alice stared at Faye. What in the world was she talking about?

"You and Bear need to watch your backs, Alice. Brendan's gone off the deep end this time. To listen to him, you would think you and Bear were the devil incarnate. And some of his fool followers are buying it. They truly believe you are out to kill the children of Poplar Point."

Alice couldn't decide if she was more shocked by what Faye was saying or by the fact that Faye, Brendan's wife, was saying it. "I don't understand, Faye. How could Brendan think that? He's known me my whole life!"

"Sometimes people need to believe they have a calling—a purpose greater than themselves. If none appears, they make one up. Me. I'm done with all that. No calling. No purpose. No Jesus waiting to save me. Nope, I'm just waiting for my exit sign. Just don't want you to see yours before you're ready."

"Faye, are you OK? I'm not sure what you're talking about, but I'm worried about you."

"Oh, I'm fine. Never been better. Are you OK?" With that, Faye walked off. When she got to the edge of the yard, she stopped and turned. "You know I've tried, don't you, Alice?" Then she continued on, disappearing into the shadow of the night.

CHAPTER 31

BEAR

WHAT A NIGHT! BEAR HEAVED a huge sigh of relief as he popped the top on a can of Heady Topper. He rolled a joint and settled back in his lounger to watch a bit of sports on TV. Just as his muscles let down, he heard a car's tires spin in the gravel outside the trailer. Oh, shit!

Bear turned off the TV and got down on his hands and knees. He crawled across the floor, picking his way through the dirty clothes and empty pizza boxes until he reached the long side window. Cautiously, he lifted one corner of the blinds, moving as slowly as he could, his hand shaking slightly. What was he going to do if Marty showed up? He had no plan. Why hadn't he made a plan? At least put the police on his speed dial and kept his phone charged? Or bought another lock for the door?

He lifted one eye carefully to the small opening he had created. At first, he could see nothing but black. A black car and someone who seemed to be dressed all in black standing on his small stoop. His heart racing, he tried to remember where he had put his phone.

Then he heard it. "Anybody got a drink around here?" Kim! Well, that was damn unexpected. Still on his hands and knees, Bear gave the trailer a quick once–over. In less than the second it took to turn his head, he knew it was beyond salvaging unless he had some time. Which he clearly didn't. Kim sounded like she was crying.

Bear clumsily got to his feet and pulled the door open. "Kim! What are you doing here?"

Without a word, Kim pushed through the door, threw herself into the lounger, and said, "I need a drink."

Bear had never seen Kim look so bad—not even the night Kim had found him on the sidewalk downtown. Bear quickly poured some whiskey into a glass. God, he hoped whiskey was OK. He realized he had no idea what Kim drank—or even if she drank. Kim grabbed the glass and took a giant gulp.

"Everything's such a mess," she said, wiping her eyes. "My marriage with Kevin is shit. We haven't been happy for years, and now I'm pretty sure he's cheating on me. It's like the more successful I become, the angrier Kevin becomes. I'm actually afraid of him sometimes."

Bear was at a loss for words. Sure, he would be happy to dump on Kevin. But he didn't want to be the one to tell Kim that Kevin had been hitting on all the waitresses at Sharky's.

"And then there's Mom. Having her unexpectedly move in hasn't improved the situation. She never liked Kevin, and there's always been tension between the two of us. She has helped a lot with the kids. But that stunt she pulled tonight! She had to realize it would upset me.

"I mean, how did she think I was going to feel when, out of the blue, she announced to the entire town that she wants to legalize selling pot in Poplar Point? Where did that come from? It's not like she's been sitting around smoking weed with her country club buddies! Or was it all just a way to hurt me?" Kim started to cry harder.

Bear nodded sympathetically but said nothing. What could he say about Helen? This wasn't the time to tell Kim that her mom was going into the marijuana business and that they had been secretly working together for weeks. But if he didn't tell her, how would she feel about him when she inevitably found out? They never should have gone along with Helen's insistence that she be a silent partner, although it sure had seemed like a wonderful idea at the time.

Bear knelt by the lounger and put his arms around Kim. Kim pressed her face into his shirt and nestled against him. In that moment, Bear decided that this wasn't the moment to tell Kim anything. He just wanted to be there for her.

God, holding Kim felt good. He rested his chin on top of her head, unconsciously drawing her closer as her crying subsided. Kim's arms went around his back. Memories from high school of the hours they had spent together at the abandoned shack by the pond came flooding back.

Kim pulled away slightly and tilted her head back, her red–rimmed eyes with their trails of mascara staring into his. Without thinking, Bear's mouth was on hers, kissing, caressing, gently probing. Slowly, Bear stood, pulling Kim out of the lounger to him. Bear felt himself harden. Oh God, did Kim notice? Almost in answer to his silent question, Kim pressed herself against him until there wasn't a sliver of space between them. Yes, he was sure she felt it, too. A powerful magnetic force was pulling them together. Their kisses became deeper, more insistent.

Bear forced himself to pull back. "Kimmie, are you sure you want to do this?"

"Yes," Kim whispered huskily, pulling him back toward her. Without ever totally separating, their clothes came off, each of them aching for the touch of the other's skin.

Bear led Kim across the floor strewn with dirty clothes to the small bedroom in the back of the trailer. For an instant, panic flared as Bear tried to remember how long it had been since he had washed the sheets. But things were moving too fast, and concerns over the state of the trailer vanished as quickly as they had come. At least he had taken a shower that morning.

Bear fell onto the bed, pulling Kim behind him. The bed groaned at the sudden weight. Bear didn't even notice. As he moved on top of Kim, all thought, all feeling, was consumed by the strength of the desire that overwhelmed him. She pulled him closer, closer, until finally her back arched as he entered her, her fingers digging into his back. She moaned as her hips rose to meet his.

Moments later, their passion satiated, Bear slowly rolled off of Kim, and Kim moved to rest her head comfortably on Bear's shoulder. They stared wonderingly at the stains on the low ceiling of the old trailer.

"Wow," said Kim. She rolled up onto her elbow and smiled at Bear. Her dark hair had, at some point, come down and was now cascading around her shoulders. "I guess it's kinda like riding a bike."

"Yeah, wow," said Bear, a sheepish grin on his face. "Kim, I've been dreaming about this since high school."

"Oh my God, I hope you haven't had to wait that long!" Kim poked Bear in the side. "No wonder you were in such a rush!"

"Rush? Me? In a rush? My mother always taught me not to contradict a woman in bed, but…." They both laughed.

"Somehow, Bear, that was exactly what I needed." Kim rose and started collecting her clothes, which trailed the length of the trailer.

Suddenly embarrassed, Bear pulled the sheet up to his waist and sat up, watching Kim as she started to dress. "Do you have to leave now?"

Kim paused and looked at him. "You know I do. I've got kids at home, and I'm sure my mother is home by now. And tomorrow is a school day. I wasn't ready to deal with any of this, Kevin, my mom—but I feel so much better now, stronger. Somehow, everything seems a lot clearer, and I understand what I need to do."

"About your mother, Kim," Bear began.

"I don't want to talk about her now. Let's just enjoy the moment. There will be time to talk later." Kim finished buttoning her blouse, slipped on her heels, and leaned over to give Bear a quick kiss on the mouth. "Thank you. You're a wonderful friend," she whispered in his ear, and then she was gone.

Still naked, with only a sheet wrapped around him, Bear sat in his bed in a state of shock. What the hell just happened? All these years he had pined for Kim, and then out of the blue, here she was. And it was great—beyond great. But what did any of it mean? "You're a wonderful friend?" Was that it? And what about Rose? Nothing serious had happened between them and yet Bear felt guilty.

Bear lay back down and put the pillow over his face.

CHAPTER 32

KIM

As KIM PULLED INTO THE driveway, she saw that all the downstairs lights were still blazing. Shoot. She pulled down the visor and checked herself in the mirror. After straightening her skirt and tucking in her blouse more carefully, she edged out of the car and tip–toed up the front steps.

Kevin, drink in hand, was seated in a chair in the living room, angled so that he would see her as soon as she walked in.

"Where have you been?" Kevin's voice was very controlled, but he was clearly livid.

"At a friend's."

"Male or female?"

"That's none of your business."

Kevin rose from the chair and walked menacingly toward Kim.

Kim looked him straight in the eye. "I meant what I said, Kevin. It's over between us. It has been for a long time. You know that. You need to leave."

"Me leave? Now why would I do that? You stomped off without bothering to listen to my side of the story! You think you're so high and mighty. And now, with no explanation, you come wandering in here reeking of whiskey and sex. I'm surprised you could even find anyone who would be interested in you! You're the one who should leave!" Kevin was so angry spittle literally flew out of his mouth as he spoke.

"Fine, Kevin. I'll leave." Kim, shoes in one hand, headed toward the stairs. Kevin followed her into their bedroom, where she began tossing a few clothes in a bag.

"What the hell are you doing, Kim? Have you lost your mind?"

"Keep your voice down. I don't want to wake the kids, and where's my mom?"

"In bed." Kevin paused. Kim watched as the reality of the situation dawned on him. "You can't leave!"

"Watch me."

Kevin grabbed Kim's arm, his grip like a vise. She knew from experience her arm would be black and blue by morning.

"Let go of me. You don't want to do this."

Kevin quickly let go. "But who's going to get the kids up? And get them to school? I don't even know—do they take a bus? Does someone make their lunch? And what am I going to say to your mother?"

"Guess you should have thought of all that." *Jerk.*

"OK, Kim." Kevin sat down heavily on the bed, his head in his hands. "Look, let's be realistic. Neither of us has any place to go. Let's both stay here tonight, and one of us can sleep on the pull–out in the basement. We can talk about this tomorrow."

"Fine, grab your stuff. There are pillows and a blanket in the closet." Kevin picked a few items out of the closet and headed for the door. As he left, he stuck his head back in and said, "We need some counseling." Kim rolled her eyes.

The door clicked shut, and Kim sat back on the bed. She was exhausted, but also exhilarated. Kevin had been berating her for years and had recently taken to physically intimidating her, shoving her. And she had let him, so afraid her marriage was unraveling.

She was glad things had finally come to a head. She didn't love Bear, never would, but he had been just what she needed to accept that her marriage was over. That it wasn't all her fault.

Suddenly Kim froze. Oh my God, what had she done? What was Bear thinking? Had she given him the impression this was something more than it was?

CHAPTER 33

KIM

THANK GOD! THE SECOND TOWN Meeting was over, and they could finally start getting back to normal—whatever that was. Kim packed all her papers in her briefcase and turned to the other Board members.

"Well, that was kind of anti–climactic," she noted.

"Thank goodness," said the Town Clerk. "I'm not sure the town could have stood another Town Meeting like the last one!"

"Yeah, that one was pretty much hell on wheels," chimed in another Board member. "I still haven't gotten over the old folks walking in at the end. I am a little surprised, though, that the vote in favor was so lop–sided. It looks like we're all in the pot business now!"

Kim tried to hide her grimace.

What a hell of a week it had been. Telling Kevin he had to leave—at least for a while until they sorted things out. Breaking the news to Emma and Ben, both of whom seemed to take it in stride. But then, who really knew what kids were thinking?

Then there was her mother. She had avoided her all week, too emotionally exhausted by all the scenes with Kevin to deal with her.

Kim pasted a smile on her face and shook hands with the other Board members, thanking them, and promising to be in touch soon about next steps.

She bolted out the back door of the Town Hall, gratefully breathing in the cool air. As she clicked the Tahoe key fob, she noticed a dark figure standing next to the car. Oh, God—it was her mother. She had seen her at the meeting, but at least this time she had stayed quiet. Thank God for small miracles.

"Kim, we have to talk." Helen stepped forward, effectively blocking Kim's path to the car door. "There are some things I need to explain."

"Not now, Mom. As I'm sure you've figured out, this has not been my best week. I'm honestly not interested in your new views on marijuana. And I need to get home and relieve the babysitter before the kids go to bed."

"Come on, Kim. We need to talk, and I checked on Emma and Ben before I left and they're fine. Putting this conversation off won't make it any easier."

Kim closed her eyes and sighed. "Oh, all right—get in the car. But hurry. I don't have much time."

Kim hit the clicker, and they both climbed in, tucking their skirts around their knees. They turned in their seats to face each other.

"Kim, since your dad left—well, I've been a bit at loose ends. I know it's been hard having me arrive on your doorstep with little forewarning, but there wasn't any place else for me to go. I've tried to be helpful, but I can understand that my moving in might have been an added strain you didn't need. I'm ready to look for an apartment. All you have to do is say the word."

Kim looked at her mother in surprise. "Really? You're asking me this *now*, Mom? With Kevin leaving and two kids at home? I gave up my child care, and it's not like I can find someone overnight! And are you thinking you want to stay in Poplar Point?"

"Well, yes. Maybe. But that's not what I wanted to talk to you about," continued Helen. "This is going to sound kind of strange—it sounds kind of strange to me, too. But I have been helping Alice and Bear work on the marijuana store idea."

"What?" Kim couldn't control the near shriek at the end of her exclamation. She looked closely at her mother to see if perhaps she was kidding. Or if she seemed like she was developing dementia—or some other kind of mental illness. Her mom stared back calmly, a hint of trepidation in her eyes.

"To be clearer, I guess it's more accurate to say we are partners. I had planned on being a silent partner, but that didn't work out."

"You mean because you couldn't control yourself and just had to stand up and make a fool of yourself—and me—at the Town Meeting?" Kim saw her mother's face redden.

"Well, that—and it turns out that legally I can't keep my role hidden either."

"But why are you doing this? How can you do this?! You hate Alice! And you told me you were seeing someone and helping them!"

"I never said that, Kim; you did. But you are right about Alice. That *is* the tricky part. Even so, somehow it all made sense. Bear had the connections, Alice had the building and some money, and I had the business know–how and needed a job. The more I've learned, the more I honestly believe legalizing marijuana is a good thing for Poplar Point—from a traditional conservative point of view, that is."

Kim stared at her mother. This was the equivalent of Genghis Khan becoming a disciple of Gandhi! Who *was* this woman?

Then, like a bolt of lightning, it struck Kim. Bear. Bear had known of his mother's involvement all along, even while he was "comforting" her after her breakdown following the last Town Meeting.

Kim had been avoiding Bear. She had been plagued by guilt. Worried that she had taken advantage of him. She had always liked Bear, and she truly did care about him as a friend. One summer in high school, she had even thought it might be something more than that. But it hadn't been, and she had moved on. She knew Bear had been disappointed, and she had suspected for a long time that he still felt something more for her. Knowing that and knowing that she could never fully reciprocate his feelings, she never should have gone to his trailer. Still, how could he not have told her about her mother? He had to have known how she would feel. What a mess.

"Mom, I don't understand any of this. This whole thing seems completely out of character for you."

"Well, maybe I'm just discovering my 'character.'"

"Yeah, right. I guess we're all 'discovering ourselves' right now. Well, I don't have time for this. I have to get home."

Helen's phone pinged. She glanced down briefly. "I know, Kim. I wanted you to know I am truly sorry if I've made it harder for you. Anyway, I've got to go, too. Let's try to talk some more soon."

"Sure, Mom." Helen opened the door. Kim watched as her mother walked hurriedly down the street toward the center of town. *Now where is she off to?* thought Kim as she slowly pulled out of the parking lot.

CHAPTER 34

BEAR

Bear was ecstatic. The meeting had gone so much better than they had even hoped! He found the Poplar Point Safe Access team, all of whom—except for Helen—were still in the hall, high–fiving and congratulating each other. A powerful feeling of affection and gratitude spread through him.

Bear spied his mother on the other side of the room, talking animatedly with Millie and Bill. He knew his mother had been a reluctant team member, but, to her credit, once committed, she had thrown herself into the fight. Now he, his mom, and Helen had to bring their dream—or some yet–to–be determined combination of their dreams—to fruition. And he had to tell them about Rose. Rose would be a great addition to their team. A flash of guilt burned through Bear as he thought of Kim. They hadn't spoken since the night of the last Town Meeting.

"Millie, any chance you want to open up for a round of celebratory beers?"

"Why, Bear, I was thinking the same thing myself!"

Cheers broke out all around. The group made its way out of the Town Hall and two blocks down the street to Millie's, their lively conversation and laughter filling the night air. Bear fired off a text to Helen. As soon as they walked in, Millie set some candles on their regular table and everyone settled into their seats with two extra chairs now added for Helen and Matt.

Once the pitchers of beer had made their rounds, Bill pounded his mug on the table and stood. "I want to make a toast to Bear for getting this motley crew together. I'm still not exactly clear how I got myself into this, but I'm sure glad to be here!" Everyone applauded.

"The time for feigned innocence has passed, Bill!" shouted Jed. Bill grinned.

Bear stood. "And I want to make a toast to my mom. None of this would have been possible without her." Bear raised his glass to his mom, followed by everyone else at the table. Alice beamed.

Just then, Helen rushed in the door. Bear raised his glass again. "And a toast, of course, to our not–so–silent partner, Helen. Thank you for keeping us all on the straight and narrow!"

"Hear, hear!" chimed the group. Helen looked embarrassed, but incredibly pleased.

"Now, as for you, Matt, the pressure's on! We gotta deliver, man!"

Bear was quite proud of himself for having shifted some of the responsibility—or at least feeling he had. He was beat.

CHAPTER 35

ALICE

As the celebration rolled on, Alice saw Rose beckon to Millie from the kitchen. Millie slipped from the room, and Alice could see the two women talking quietly. Rose was clearly upset about something.

Alice glanced around the table. None of the men had noticed—no surprise there. And Helen was too busy basking in her new–found glory to be keeping track of anyone else's movements.

Alice carefully pushed her chair back, trying not to attract any attention, and walked over to Millie and Rose. "What's wrong? Anything I can do to help?"

Millie looked at Rose, who nodded. "Alice," began Millie, "Rose has gotten some troubling news, and we need to keep this to ourselves for now while we figure out what to do."

"OK. How about if Millie and I get things to wrap up here, Rose, and then we can have a good talk?"

Rose nodded tearfully and moved further back into the kitchen, out of sight.

Alice and Millie walked back out and stood next to the table. Eventually, Bill noticed them and astutely picked up the signal. "Well, guys, this sure has been a great evening, but I've gotta be heading home." As Bill pushed his chair back, the rest of the group followed suit, everyone grabbing sweaters and jackets while they continued to chatter and move toward the door.

Bear turned. "Ma, you coming?"

"Not yet. I'm gonna stay here and help Millie clean up."

"OK. Millie, thanks! Send me a bill in a few months and I'll be good for it!"

"Let's hope so." said Bill, leading the parade out the door.

As soon as everyone was gone, Rose came out of the kitchen with three steaming cups of tea on a tray and the women sat together at a clean table. Alice noticed immediately that Rose had been crying. "Oh, Rose, what's wrong?"

Rose plunged right in. "I've made some bad decisions in my life, Alice, and the worst one was marrying a guy out in Denver named Tony. We had only been married a week when the abuse started. It got pretty bad—a broken collar bone, black eyes, bruises, the whole nine yards. So, one day while Tony was at work, I left and moved into a women's shelter. They helped me get a restraining order, which unfortunately was of no use at all."

Alice shook her head sadly and inched her chair closer to Rose's.

"Tony claimed I'd ruined his life. He was adamant that I had to come back to him so that he could prove everything was all right between us and that *he* hadn't done anything wrong. I didn't go back, but each time I left the shelter, he would find me and the violence would start all over again."

Alice took Rose's hand. "I'm so sorry, Rose. No one deserves that. How did you finally get away?"

"After a particularly bad beating, I called the police and Tony was arrested and ultimately convicted of violating the restraining order and of assault. He went to prison. As soon as the trial was over, I packed a small bag, stole an old motorcycle out of the garage, and made it to a shelter in Boston. I figured distance was my best chance at protecting myself." Rose shifted uncomfortably in her chair.

"Tonight, after the Town Meeting, I picked up a message on my phone from my counselor in Boston. She was calling to tell me they'd gotten a call from a shelter in Denver saying Tony was out and looking for me. He doesn't have any idea where I am, but still, I'm so afraid." Rose put her head down on her arms and started to cry.

Alice and Millie both leaned over and put their arms around Rose's shoulders.

"That bastard," Alice said under her breath. "From what you know of Tony, Rose, do you think he'd come as far as the East Coast trying to find you?"

"I'm afraid so, Alice. If he was angry before about my ruining his life, I can only imagine how he feels now that he's been in prison *and* I've filed for divorce. Really, I have ruined his life."

"No, Rose," said Alice. "You did *not* ruin Tony's life; Tony did. And now you're not alone. You've got Millie and Bear and me. We'll be standing right beside you, making sure he doesn't cause you any more trouble."

Rose looked up. "But how are we going to do that?"

Alice and Millie traded concerned looks.

"Do you have any family we should call, Rose?" asked Alice.

"No. My dad, who was pretty abusive himself, died when I was ten. My mom and I went to live with my grandparents. But they're all dead now."

"Well, we're your family now, and we'll figure it out," Alice said reassuringly, patting Rose's hand.

Millie nodded. "Rose is going to go back up to Boston, Alice. Just to get some advice, nudge the divorce proceeding along, and see what else she can learn about Tony."

"Sounds like a good idea," said Alice. She turned to Rose. "Does Bear know?"

"He knows I was married and that I'm getting a divorce, but he doesn't know all the rest of the details."

"You should tell him, Rose, so he's got the full picture."

"I know." Rose blew her nose, squared her shoulders, and got up. "Listen, you two, don't worry about me. I'll be all right. I've been through worse, and now I have you and Bear." Rose put on a brave smile as she began clearing beer mugs and pretzel bags off the table.

Alice stood and began helping. She was devastated. Just when things were starting to look up, why was life so damn hard?

PART 2

Six Months Later

CHAPTER 36

ALICE

"ALICE, ARE YOU HOME?" HELEN knocked impatiently on the screened door, then gave it a push, crossing the porch with a determined stride. "Alice! I have a brilliant idea!"

Alice slowly walked in from the kitchen, wet dishtowel in hand, hair spilling out of the loose pile on top of her head. "Uh–oh. Now what, Helen? If this involves more meetings...."

"No, no. This is about fun—and work."

Alice looked at Helen skeptically, not too sure their definitions of fun would have much in common. "OK—shoot."

"Well, I've heard you say to Bear that you would like to visit some aunt in Omaha, particularly now that she's getting on in years. As for me, we've been working so hard for the past six months I'm pretty burned out. I'm guessing you are too, given your recent pot consumption." Helen laughed at her joke, quite pleased with herself. "So, I was thinking maybe the two of us could fly out to Colorado for a little business recon, then stop by your aunt's on the way back."

"Business recon?" Alice wasn't sure what Helen was talking about. "I don't know, Helen. I'm not much of a traveler. Last time I was on a plane they still had stewardesses with cute little hats. Besides, how much would this cost?"

"Not as much as you think, Alice. I've talked it over with Matt, and he thinks visiting some of the established stores in the Denver area would be a great way for us get a better feel for how a cannabis dispensary operates and what we like and don't like. He's even promised to put together a questionnaire that we can use to prepare for visiting the stores. Plus, Colorado is gorgeous in the spring."

Alice started to shake her head, trying to picture the two of them on some mutually enjoyable trip that involved reconnoitering pot stores in Colorado.

"Oh, come on, Alice. Pleaaaaasssse. I don't want to do this by myself. And it would be good for both of us to get out of Poplar Point for a little while."

Alice considered Helen. Frankly, she was a little surprised that Helen would want to go on a trip with her. True, they had been doing pretty well together and had managed to avoid any major blow–ups for several months now. But at least part of the explanation for that was that they all had been so darn busy—getting legal with the state, reaching agreements with all the arms of the town, drawing up plans for the renovation of Arlo's old store, and, of course, stealing Rose away from Millie's. They had spent very little time just the two of them.

But then Alice thought about Helen. This was the first time since Jack left that Helen had shown any enthusiasm for anything other than work and her grandchildren, let alone something "fun." They never talked about it, but Helen must still be very hurt by Jack's betrayal. And, as far as she could tell, Helen didn't have any other friends she could go on a trip with. Truth be told, Alice needed a break, too. But with Helen? Could they possibly put up with each other long enough to get to Colorado and back? Alice wasn't sure.

"I'm not sure this is the right time, Helen. The renovations to the store are about done, and there's still so much to do if we're ever going to open."

"That's why we have Bear and Rose, Alice! And I'm sure they wouldn't mind some time to themselves."

"OK. I'll think about it."

"Great! Here's your e–ticket. We leave Tuesday and we'll only be gone a week. You call your aunt and tell her we'll be in Omaha on the 26th for one night. You can decide whether we should stay with her or book a place. I've made all the other arrangements. Bye! Gotta go. Got a hair appointment in 15 minutes."

Helen rushed out the door without so much as a glance back. Alice stood in the living room, mouth slightly agape, with an e–ticket in her hand. God God, now what had she gotten herself into!

CHAPTER 37

BEAR

Bear walked briskly out of Friendly's Market, a six–pack under one arm, a bag of chips and some dip in the other, and a grin on his face. At last, the weekend was here, and he and Rose were heading out to Jed and Chrissie's. He dumped everything in the back seat, then hopped in the front of the truck. After checking for cars, he reached down to turn on the radio as he began backing out of the parking space. *Crunch!* Bear's head snapped up. Damn! Where did that car come from?

Bear fished his registration and insurance card out of the glove compartment and climbed out of the truck. A dark blue Tahoe was a foot behind him, the rear panel dented. Shit! He knew the car.

"What the hell, Bear? Did you look where you were going?" Kim swung herself out of the Tahoe's high driver's seat and straightened her skirt.

"Of course I looked! Did you?"

They stood in the parking lot, glaring at each other, somewhat at a loss for where to go next.

"Hey, mister, can you move your truck?"

Bear and Kim got back into their large vehicles, one quite new and shiny, the other basically a piece of junk with a hunting rifle hanging in the back window, and edged back into their respective spaces. Then they climbed back out to face each other again.

"Kim, about your mother ..."

"What? You just rammed into my car and you want to talk about my mother?"

"No, I don't want to talk about your mother, but we've been avoiding each other for six months now and I think we need to talk."

"Do you have insurance?"

"Of course I have insurance. Do you?"

Kim huffed and began searching in her bag for her wallet.

"Come on, Kim. I wanted to tell you about your mother that night. I even started to once. But you were so upset. I just couldn't get it out."

"Well, I seem to recall you getting something else out just fine."

Bear reddened. "And I seem to recall having a little help."

By now, several folks had stopped on the cement walk in front of Friendly's to listen. Entertainment was pretty hard to come by in Poplar Point, even on a Friday night.

Bear cautiously walked closer to Kim so they could keep their voices down. "Look, Kim. I'm sorry about your car. We'll get that sorted. But I'm kind of glad this happened so we have a chance to talk."

"Are you saying you hit me on purpose?"

"Of course not!" Bear took a deep breath and counted to ten. "OK. I am going to try this one more time. Kim, I'm sorry I didn't tell you about your mother. I can imagine you were upset when you found out. But I never meant to hurt you. We've been friends a long time. I cared about you then, and I care about you now. I know you've been dealing with a lot, and I'd rather that we not look back at what happened between us with regret."

Kim stared at her shoes. Finally, she looked up. "You're right, Bear. I have been avoiding you. It was probably inevitable we'd run into each other sooner or later."

"Ha ha."

Kim gave a half smile. "A lot of things weren't right that night. You should have told me about my mother. And I probably shouldn't have come to you in the first place, given the state I was in."

"Well, some things went pretty right, Kim, and I don't think either of us should go around regretting it or feeling like we're afraid to run into each other. Let's focus on the positive and get back to being friends again."

Kim raised an eyebrow and looked at Bear.

"Just friends—without benefits," Bear amended.

"Deal."

Kim and Bear stared at each other for a minute, then sighed, the first traces of smiles appearing. They passed their registrations and insurance cards to each other and got out their phones.

CHAPTER 38

BEAR

BEAR PULLED AWAY FROM THE airport on Tuesday, feeling lighter than he had in months. He flipped on the radio to his favorite bluegrass station and sang along in an off–key voice as he slogged his way through Boston's tunnels and usual snarled traffic back to Rose and Poplar Point.

Bear laughed to himself as he thought of his mom and Helen walking into the airport—Helen fashionably dressed in a black pantsuit and comfortable heels, pulling her set of three matched suitcases. And his mom in her usual hippie attire, with sensible shoes and a backpack on her back, water bottle attached. Helen had clearly been appalled by his mother's choice of luggage, but had not said a word. Maybe this was progress! Even so, this was a trip he was not sorry to miss.

Bear finally pulled into the lot by the store, tooted the horn, then climbed out of the truck. Rose appeared at the side door, her usual perch for overseeing the renovation going on inside. She ran to Bear and threw her arms around his chest, her fingers meeting in the back.

"Did they get off?"

"As far as I know. I turned my phone off when they left." Bear grinned from ear to ear. "So, is everything under control here?"

"I think so. Why? What do you have in mind?" Rose poked Bear in the side playfully.

"Gee, I dunno." Bear tucked Rose's arm through his and they started a slow stroll around the old building.

"It's lookin' real good, Bear. They finished the electrical work this morning. Now we get to the fun part—sanding the floors, painting, installing display cases, shelves, racks, and, of course, the wood stove."

"Rose, we never would have been able to do all this without you." Bear bent down to give her a lingering kiss on the lips. "Don't you think it's about time we went public?"

Rose hesitated, then raised her eyes. "Honestly, Bear, it's not like everyone doesn't know we're together. I'm sure Millie has noticed that I haven't slept in my room for weeks. And we work around your mom and Helen every day. They're not blind. We don't need a formal announcement or anything."

Bear wrapped her in his arms. "I know. It's just that I'm so happy. I want to tell everyone about it."

"Who knew you were such a talker?" Rose pulled back from Bear and took his hands. "Seriously, Bear, the divorce is taking longer than I would have liked. It's a little complicated making sure that Tony can't get any information about where I am. And it's been difficult tracking down Tony. Millie's been a tremendous help talking with the lawyer in Denver."

Bear frowned. "And you're sure Tony doesn't know where you are?"

A shiver ran down Rose's back.

CHAPTER 39

HELEN

After waiting for more than an hour, Helen and Alice finally were boarding their flight. Row 17, seats A and B. Helen was ecstatic. Come hell or high water, she was going to enjoy herself after months of feeling like she had been dropped into someone else's life.

"Alice, do you mind if I take the window seat?"

"Of course not. Make yourself comfortable."

Helen settled herself in her seat, then watched as Alice first attempted to squash her backpack under the seat in front of her, then tried to lift it into the overhead compartment. Just as Helen was considering whether she should try to help, an arm reached around Alice to support the backpack. "Here, let me get that for you, ma'am."

Helen turned to see a tall older gentleman in a well–pressed checkered shirt and jeans with a cowboy hat pulled low over his forehead. "Yes, thank you. That would be great," Alice mumbled in a rush. Alice struggled into the middle seat as the man easily hefted the backpack into the overhead bin, then followed it with a small black leather case of his own. He squeezed into the seat next to Alice, his knees half–way up the back of the seat in front of him. As Alice settled herself, Helen reached across her for her seatbelt. "Stop that, Helen," Alice whispered sharply, slapping Helen's hand lightly. "I've got it."

Helen leaned back in her seat and turned to face out the window. Alice seemed so unworldly and unsophisticated, but Helen knew she had to rein herself in if they were going to get along. Good grief, they were both in their sixties and surely capable of taking care of themselves.

Helen reached into her large shoulder bag and withdrew her Kindle. Slipping on a pair of Calvin Klein reading glasses, she began to read. Two minutes later, she looked up in annoyance. Didn't Alice know the first rule of travel? Never make eye contact or you may end up stuck in a conversation you have no interest in for the next four hours. Yet here was Alice, chattering happily to the man next to her like they were long–lost best friends.

Helen surreptitiously glanced at the man out of the corner of her eye. He seemed nice enough, but what was the deal with all the Western get–up? She noted the well–worn cowboy boots and wind–burned face. What could he possibly be talking to Alice about?

Helen went back to her reading, but couldn't help overhearing pieces of their conversation.

"So, what do you do, Dan?"

"Nothing terribly exciting, I'm afraid. I'm a lawyer."

A lawyer? Helen was surprised. He certainly didn't look like any lawyer she had ever seen. He'd probably gone to some second–rate law school out West and hung out a shingle in some cow town.

"Well, I hope you're not a Fed," said Alice, a sly smile on her face. Helen cringed.

"Nope."

"That's a relief. Then I can tell you what Helen and I have been up to.

CHAPTER 40

ALICE

As the plane began its descent into Denver, Alice took a break from her conversation with Dan to lean forward and peer around Helen out the window. Wow! Her first glimpse of the Rockies and weren't they something! The snow–covered peaks sparkling in the bright spring sunlight made for a stark contrast with the dark purples and greens of the lower slopes. And there, edging into view, was a series of enormous modernistic white teepees. Why, that must be the airport. Certainly a far cry from Boston's old dump, Logan. The first wave of excitement hit Alice. Maybe this was a good idea.

After an impressively smooth landing, rewarded by a quick round of applause, the chaos of getting all the bags out of the overhead bins began. Dan easily reached Alice's backpack and placed it on his seat, then grabbed his black bag and doffed his cowboy hat.

"Nice talkin' with you, Alice. I'll give you a call tomorrow." And Dan was off. After waiting for Helen to scour the area around their seats looking for anything they might have dropped, Alice moved into the aisle, made a space for Helen, and then trailed Helen off the plane to baggage claim.

Helen's bags were soon loaded onto a cart, and the two women headed toward the door. As they walked outside, Helen explained to Alice that they were looking for the Hertz shuttle that would take them to their car rental. Alice dutifully marched along after Helen, much like a child on a school holiday—excited, but slightly irritated at having to follow her parent. Alice caught herself, mentally paused, and reminded herself how grateful she was to Helen for having organized everything for them.

As they lugged the bags onto the rental shuttle, Alice was struck by the sea of cowboy hats and other Western gear on the bus. It was a bit like landing on the set of Yellowstone! She took a seat next to Helen and then glanced up at the sign posted above the heads of the passengers across the aisle warning about forgotten firearms. Good thing Helen hadn't brought her gun. Or who knew, maybe they would wish she had!

Alice waited with the luggage while Helen went to the Hertz counter. An eternity later, Helen returned. "Come on, Alice," Helen said brightly, jingling a set of keys in her right hand. "Let's hit the road!"

Feeling somewhat like a Himalayan Sherpa, Alice grabbed two bags and followed Helen into the garage. She looked on aghast as Helen clicked the key fob and the lights lit up on a black Lincoln Navigator with tinted windows.

"Helen! This car is enormous! It looks like a drug dealer's car!"

"No, Alice. It looks like a rich person's car."

"Is there any difference?"

Helen turned and gave Alice a warning look. "Just get in."

Alice walked around to the back of the car to load the bags. Gazing into the SUV's interior reminded Alice more of looking at someone's living room than a car. Helen certainly liked things *big*. She'd have to remember to ask her about that.

As she loaded the suitcases in the back, Alice was momentarily paralyzed by guilt. She had already blown her carbon neutrality goal for the month with her cross–country flight, and here she was about to take off in this gas–guzzling beast! Alice pushed a button and the back gate silently closed, ending with an almost inaudible click. Still somewhat disgusted but resigned to her fate, Alice walked around the side of the car, opened the heavy passenger door, and climbed in. At least they had a place to stay if the hotel wasn't up to Helen's standards.

Forty–five minutes later, they arrived at their hotel, a large, expensive–looking establishment in downtown Denver. As she clambered out of the car, Alice took in the hotel's elaborate facade and the doorman standing at the gold–plated entrance. Alice knew better than to expect Motel 6 with Helen, but this exceeded all expectations. "Helen, are you sure we're at the right place? This is awfully fancy."

"Don't worry, Alice. I used the points on Jack's and my old credit card. We have a suite with two bedrooms which should be perfect for us. I think you're going to love it. There's an indoor pool and a spa that gets a great write–up in Condé Nast. This is going to be so much fun."

Alice watched dubiously as Helen climbed gracefully out of the driver's seat, handed the keys to the waiting attendant, and strode up the steps toward the lobby. Alice followed from behind with her backpack, feeling like she should have had a piece of straw or perhaps a toothpick sticking out from between her teeth.

After Helen filled out the registration card and got their room keys, a bellman accompanied them to the elevator and up to their suite. Alice wanted to snatch her backpack from its new incongruous perch on top of Helen's neatly stacked matched set of luggage.

Alice observed the bellman carefully as he held the room keycard against a metal box on the door and then opened the door for them. The suite was beautiful, all blue–grays and muted golds with recessed lighting. Alice had never seen anything like it. She would have to take some pictures to send to Bear when Helen wasn't looking. Or would that seem too materialistic? What was she doing in a place like this, anyway? A wave of homesickness unexpectedly swept over her.

Meanwhile, Helen was bustling about, checking the bathrooms, the mini bars, the closets. Thankfully, everything checked out. Helen whipped out a $10 bill and handed it to the bellman as he left. *Good grief—ten dollars!*

As the door closed, Helen turned to Alice. "So, what do you think?" Helen was beaming.

"It's nice, Helen—really nice. It just seems like more than we need."

Helen laughed. "Come on, Alice, relax. We deserve this after the past six months!"

Alice watched as Helen flung herself into a dark gray and aqua upholstered lounge chair and kicked off her shoes. She appeared more comfortable than Alice had seen her since she'd returned to Poplar Point. Might be just what the doctor ordered.

Alice settled herself in a leather recliner across the room. "By the way, Helen, Dan has invited us to dinner our last night here. And it turns out one of his nephews owns a high–end cannabis store on the outskirts of Denver. He's offered to call and arrange for us to meet him if we want." Alice, who was quite pleased with herself for having made these connections, was surprised by Helen's reaction.

"Dan who?" Helen scoffed. "You don't know anything about him. Or about his nephew, for that matter."

"Actually, I do. Dan and I spent several hours talking while you kept your nose buried in your fake book with your headphones plastered to your ears so you wouldn't have to interact with anyone."

"I prefer not to converse with strangers on planes. And why would you agree to go to dinner with a man you don't even know? It's not like you're ever going to see him again."

"I enjoyed talking to him, so why not? It's not like he's an axe murderer or anything."

"How do you know? Anyway, I'm not going. By the way, I'm booking myself a facial and a mani–pedi for tomorrow night. Do you want anything?"

"You're booking a what?"

"A mani–pedi. Really, Alice. It's what people call a manicure and a pedicure. You do know what those are, don't you?"

"No massage?" Alice couldn't resist.

"Very funny. But you should book yourself one."

"I may need one. I've put together quite a list of stores for us to visit, and we are going to be busy! If it's OK with you, I'm going to go take a shower and order up a salad."

"Sounds perfect," agreed Helen.

Alice got up and headed toward her room. As she entered the doorway, she paused and turned back, remembering again her pledge to be grateful. "Thank you again for doing all this, Helen. This hotel really is something."

Alice closed the door behind her, plopped her backpack on the luggage rack, and laid herself out on the sumptuous pillow–top, her legs dangling off the side. She unwrapped a piece of mint chocolate that was lying on the bed and popped it into her mouth. Not bad, although she would have preferred an edible with a little more oomph.

CHAPTER 41

ALICE

Alice woke up early the next day and pulled open the black–out curtains in her room. It was a glorious spring day. The air was crystal clear, providing breathtaking vistas of mountains that seemed almost within reach outside the window. Alice felt better than she had in days!

After a few moments in the bathroom, Alice walked out into the main room of the suite, dug through her backpack and the mini-fridge, and settled herself at the table. Within moments, Helen quietly slipped out of her room, clearly unaware that Alice was already up.

"Good God, Helen! You look like a dead panda bear. What the hell is that stuff on your face?"

Helen jumped at the sound of Alice's voice, then frowned. "It's a masque, silly. I'm getting ready for my facial this evening."

"Why do you have to get ready? I thought the facial was supposed to fix your skin?"

"Fix?" Helen scowled, but then waved her hand in the air as though swatting an annoying insect away. "What did you find for breakfast, Alice?"

"I have some kefir and a few energy bars I brought. Help yourself."

"I won't even bother to ask." Helen headed back to her room, calling back over her shoulder. "Let's get dressed and head out. We can pick up something to eat on the way to the first store."

"Sounds good. I can be ready in five."

Alice heard Helen laugh as she closed the door. "See you in an hour."

An hour and a half later, Alice and Helen's taxi pulled up in front of the Denver Green Superstore. Although they had considered driving, Helen had decided against it, modestly pointing out to Alice that parking the Navigator in downtown Denver might be difficult, even given her excellent parallel parking skills.

Helen paid the driver, and they both climbed out of the taxi. They stood on the sidewalk, staring up at the surprisingly imposing store, suddenly unsure of their next steps.

"Oh, come on. It's only a store," grumbled Helen as she led the way in, pulling Matt's list of questions out of her bag as she went. "We've got this."

A young man immediately greeted them. "Can I help you?"

"Why, yes. We'd like to speak to the manager, please," replied Helen.

Alice's eyebrows shot up. "The manager, Helen?"

Helen waved a hand at Alice, as though shushing her. "Yes, the manager."

The young man was a bit taken aback. "You sure you need to see the manager, ma'am? Is there a problem?"

"No. We're opening a dispensary in Massachusetts and were hoping to talk to your manager about his experiences."

"Well, *she* isn't here right now. But why don't I introduce you to Doug, one of our most experienced bud tenders?"

Alice answered immediately, cutting Helen off at the pass. "That would be great." As the young man walked away, Alice turned quickly. "Helen," she whispered, "I don't think we need to demand to see the manager. I thought we were just casually checking things out."

"I am not *demanding* anything. It's just that in my experience, it's always best to start at the top."

Alice fidgeted as they waited, clearly uncomfortable with Helen's somewhat imperious approach. Moments later, another young man approached, hand extended. "Hi, I'm Doug. How can I help you ladies today?"

Helen shook hands crisply and without waiting for Alice to introduce herself, announced, "Before we start, I just want to say that I don't use marijuana or any drugs for that matter. We are just here to discuss business."

"Helen! What are you doing?" Alice looked aghast.

"So let me get this clear," said Doug. "You don't use any drugs, you don't have any interest in buying any cannabis products, but you want to talk about our business?" Doug looked both annoyed and suspicious. Alice jumped in.

"Actually, unlike my friend Helen here, I am definitely interested in purchasing a few of your top products, Doug. Helen and I are working together with a team opening one of the first recreational dispensaries in Massachusetts. We both totally get the importance of quality product, as well as a store's vibe and mission. We're just trying to learn from others' experiences. Tell us what do you like most about the Superstore, Doug?"

Helen's eyes flashed. "Actually, I was more interested in your cash strategies and your POS and inventory management software."

As Doug stared uncomfortably at the two women, the security guard made his way over. "Need any help, bro?"

Doug shook his head, as Alice and Helen stared at each other.

"Hmm … guess we should have coordinated a bit more," said Helen.

"Ya think?"

Doug recovered quickly. "Shauna," he called across the floor to another bud tender. "Can you show Alice around for a bit? I'm gonna take Helen here back to talk to Derrick if he's available. Helen, follow me. Derrick's our IT guy and I think you might enjoy meeting him."

A young woman with long straight brown hair, skinny jeans and a heavily-embroidered peasant top approached Alice. Instant rapport having been established, they walked off toward the flower display, chatting happily.

Half an hour later, Alice saw Helen walking out from the back offices accompanied by a ginormous man with a shaved round head and multiple tattoos covering his arms and hands. Alice's gaze shifted worriedly to Helen, but Helen, much to Alice's relief, appeared perfectly relaxed. Helen stopped and turned to Derrick, holding out her hand. "Thanks, Derrick. That was so helpful."

"My pleasure, Helen. Hope to see you around. Call me anytime."

Helen walked briskly toward Alice, her eyes lighting on the two small shopping bags hanging from Alice's arm. "I see you've been busy, Alice."

Alice laughed lightly. “Just doin’ a little product research, Helen.” As they walked out the front door, Alice turned to Helen. “So, how’d it go with Derrick?”

“Great,” replied Helen as she jauntily waved her hand for a taxi. “He was a fount of good information, Alice, and I think he really enjoyed talking to someone who was interested in hearing about what he does, as opposed to just which cannabis strain gives you the best high.”

Alice frowned.

Helen glanced again at the shopping bags. “You know, Alice, if you feel compelled to buy something at every store we visit, you’re going to have an awful lot of marijuana.”

“Just let me worry about that,” said Alice as the two women slid into the back seat of a bright yellow taxi and sped off across town.

CHAPTER 42

ALICE

SEVERAL NIGHTS LATER, ALICE SWIPED her keycard and quietly let herself into the hotel room. She had hoped Helen was already in bed so she would be spared the twenty questions, but no such luck. Helen was standing at the bar pouring a generous splash of Johnnie Walker Black into an ice–filled crystal glass.

"How was your dinner with Dan, Alice? I wasn't sure if you'd be coming home tonight."

Alice rolled her eyes. "For Pete's sake, Helen. Get real. Actually, the dinner was very nice. I've never met anyone quite like Dan before. Would you believe he used to ride in the rodeo *and* he's a big opera fan?"

"Why, he sounds like a regular Renaissance man, Alice."

"A what?"

"Oh, never mind. I'm exhausted. Aren't you?"

"You can say that again. We have covered a lot of ground these last five days. I can't believe we're leaving tomorrow!" Alice fell back into one of the lounge chairs, put her feet up, and extracted a fat pre–rolled joint from her pocket. She lit the joint and inhaled deeply, waiting for that wonderful sensation of relaxation to suffuse her body. Alice looked more closely at Helen as she walked back to her chair, glass in hand. Suddenly, she sat straight up. "Helen, what the hell happened to your face?! You haven't had a stroke, have you?"

"What are you talking about, Alice?" Helen was clearly annoyed.

"Your face! One side is different."

"Don't be ridiculous! How much have you smoked tonight?" Although she was clearly irritated, Helen dragged herself out of her chair and over to the mirror. She leaned in close, running her hand lightly down the right side of her face. "Hmm, I see what you mean. The woman who did my facial was trying to sell me some new plumping cream, and she rubbed some on the right side of my face so I could see the difference. Then another customer arrived, and I guess she finished me up without ever putting any of the cream on the left side of my face. Unbelievable! This stuff seems to really work! Remind me to go back and get some if we have time."

"I'm not even going to ask what it costs."

"No, don't." Helen sat back down and picked up her drink.

Alice resettled herself, then looked at Helen again. "Well, I hope the plump doesn't last too long. Now that that's settled, I have another question for you." Alice waved her joint at Helen. "After visiting so many cannabis stores, aren't you even the slightest bit curious?"

"A little, I guess. It's been kind of weird spending days going into all these stores, looking at different kinds of products. I've learned a lot more than I expected to, but I still have no idea what the big deal is." Helen took a good–sized sip of her drink and rose to get a refill. "And," she continued, "I have to admit, I've been a little surprised by the range of customers. I was expecting a bunch of washed–up potheads with tie–dyed tees and beads."

"You mean like me?"

"No, of course not. You know what I mean." Alice shook her head. Would she ever get used to this stupid shit from Helen? Helen continued. "There were all kinds of people, some of them quite well–dressed and normal–looking."

"Helen, do you ever think about how insulting some of the things you say are? And, honestly, nobody is suggesting you become a drug addict. But don't you think you should at least try a little so you know what you're talking about? What is it you're so afraid of? I can understand it when it's illegal. But marijuana isn't illegal here."

"I don't know, Alice. I guess I just don't like the idea of mind–altering drugs."

"You mean like scotch?" Before Helen could reply, Alice continued. "And don't tell me your martinis and scotch and white wine aren't mind–altering. Shall we talk about that evening I found you passed out on the sidewalk? You were a little altered that night, sweetie!"

Helen's cheeks reddened. "OK. Fine. But I am not going to smoke anything. And you have to promise this stays between the two of us. You are never allowed to breathe a word of this to anyone without my permission."

"Got it." Alice reached into her pocket. "I seem to recall you were quite interested in the edibles." Alice opened a cellophane bag of gummies. "Which one would you like?"

Helen stared. "Are they different?"

"Well, they're different colors. But, no, other than that, they aren't different."

Helen's frown lines deepened. "OK, just give me one." As she reached to pop it in her mouth, Alice lunged and grabbed her hand. "Alice!" Helen exclaimed. "What are you doing? I thought you wanted me to do this!"

"I do. I mean, I want you to if you want to. But, Helen, I don't have much experience with gummies. If I were you, I'd only eat half of it. You won't notice the effects for a while, and we don't have any idea how you're going to react. You could react strongly, or it might not even affect you the first time. You really should take it slow."

"Thanks for the advice, Alice. But I can handle this on my own." Helen popped the gummy in her mouth and leaned back in her chair, arranging herself comfortably and closing her eyes as she chewed. Alice, who was getting a pleasant buzz on, began again to unwind.

Thirty minutes later, Helen said, "I don't feel any different. Should I eat another one?"

"No! Just relax and give it time." Alice tried to recapture her sensation of intense relaxation. Whoa—could you be intensely relaxed? Alice suppressed a chuckle.

"Alice, did you turn the lights down?"

Alice opened one eye. "Nooo."

"And the music, it's moving. Wow! Now the lights and the music are going together. This is cool."

Just then, a siren shrieked outside their hotel window. Helen jumped out of her chair, making a beeline for her bedroom.

Slightly annoyed, Alice sat up. "Helen, where are you going?"

"They're coming. Didn't you hear that? They're coming. I have to hide." Helen continued into the bathroom off her room, and Alice could hear the shower curtain's metallic slide along the pole.

Alice resignedly hauled herself out of her chair and walked to the bathroom. "Who's coming, Helen?"

"Them. Oh, I don't know. I think it's the police. But it might be Kimberly. Oh God. What am I going to say? I know. I'll say you gave me a gummy bear, and I thought it was a piece of candy." Helen poked her head around the edge of the shower curtain. "Do I seem normal?"

"Oh, sure, Helen—other than the fact you're standing in the shower with all your clothes on."

"Oh, right." Helen concentrated, her brow furrowed, as she looked down and began the daunting task of unbuttoning her blouse. Clearly frustrated, she gave up part way down and shifted her focus to the more accommodating zipper on the side of her skirt.

"Helen, stop that. Nobody's coming, but if someone did come, you don't want to be naked—right? I mean, how would that look?" Alice's head was beginning to hurt. This was too confusing. "Helen, get out of the shower and come sit down. That's the best thing. No one is coming."

Helen rebuttoned her shirt and zipped her skirt, stepped out of the tub and began the ten–mile walk to her chair in the living room. Alice was amazed anyone could move so slowly. Helen's eyes grew wider and wider. A small smile played at her lips as she oh so carefully balanced, arms out to her side, and baby–stepped across the room. As she eased herself into her seat, she burst out laughing. "That was amazing. I boinged."

"You what?"

"I boinged. You know—like one of those stretchy clowns with springs on its feet."

Alice closed her eyes and put her hand to her forehead. Something told her this was going to be a long night. "Are you hungry?"

Helen nodded her head vigorously. "But I'm not sure I can walk to the kitchen."

"Don't worry, I've got it." Alice checked Helen out carefully. She seemed all right.

Alice returned with two bags of Doritos and ranch dip. Helen grabbed a bag out of her hand, ripping it open before it even reached her lap. She stuffed a handful into her mouth. "These are so delicious!"

Alice settled back into her chair again, munching and willing herself back into what she called her zone—a place of peace, wonder, and discovery. She shut her eyes, enjoying the journey.

A few minutes later—or was it an hour?—Alice jerked awake, remembering Helen and the promise she had made to herself that she would make sure Helen had a positive experience. She straightened up and studied Helen across the room. Helen was still sitting in her chair, back straight, eyes wide open, an empty bag of Doritos folded neatly in her lap.

"You doing OK, Helen?"

Helen nodded.

"Can I get you anything?"

Helen shook her head.

The cat must have got her tongue. Alice started laughing. What an absurd expression! How would a cat get your tongue? And what would it do with it? Alice closed her eyes and on the back of her eyelids tried to picture a cat going for Helen's tongue. Alice thought the whole thing hilarious. Laughing so hard she had tears running down her face, she attempted to explain to Helen what she found so funny. Helen just looked at her.

Wow. This is some weird shit. How many times had she wished Helen couldn't speak? And here they were! Alice started laughing again.

After rummaging in the tiny kitchen for something else to eat and sharing it with Helen, who accepted the food mutely, Alice had an overwhelming urge to lie down and go to sleep. It had been an exhausting few days. Since it seemed unlikely Helen was going to make it to her bedroom, Alice decided she better just lie down on the couch so she could keep an eye on her. Within minutes, she was snoring softly.

CHAPTER 43

HELEN

THE COLORADO SUN ROSE BRIGHT and early, sending piercing shafts of light through the half–open blinds into the living room of Helen and Alice's suite. Helen woke, surprised to find herself sitting in a chair, a Dorito bag folded neatly in her lap. Slowly, the events of the previous evening came back to her—her muteness, her paranoia, her ravenous appetite. Helen really wasn't sure why people thought this was fun. Personally, she found drinking a lot more enjoyable and certainly more predictable. She cringed as an image of herself hiding in the shower flashed through her mind. God, she hoped Alice kept this to herself! Surprisingly, though, other than a pretty stiff back she felt quite good.

Helen stared at Alice lying on the couch, one arm flung over her face, her jaw slack, a tiny line of saliva trailing down her chin. Alice really was a mess. Then again, she had slept on the couch in the living room to be sure Helen was all right.

Helen watched quietly as Alice groaned and rolled over, almost falling off the couch. Alice's eyes popped open. As she pulled herself to a sitting position, she scanned the room frantically.

"Helen, are you OK? Did you get any sleep?"

Helen shook her head and then, as though trying out words for the first time, she whispered, "I don't remember going to sleep, but I'm not really sure. I remember trying to get up and go to my room, but I was stuck. It was the weirdest thing. But now I think I'm fine."

"That was some crazy ride you took, Helen."

Helen nodded. "I guess I'm glad I tried it, but I don't think I'll be doing that again."

Alice laughed. "We'll see. We just need to get you a little more relaxed and past the paranoia thing."

"Alice, in case you haven't noticed, 'relaxed' is not a word that is commonly associated with me."

Hands braced on the arms of her chair, Helen rose shakily, a small groan escaping her lips as she straightened her back. Slowly, she made her way to her room. "Let's get this show on the road. We don't want to be late getting to Omaha, Alice! Didn't you say your aunt was expecting us for dinner? And we have a seven–and–a–half–hour drive ahead of us."

An hour later, Helen was at the reception desk in the lobby checking out while Alice watched over the luggage. As the black Lincoln pulled into the circular driveway, Alice and Helen both walked around to the driver's side.

"What are you doing, Alice?"

"I thought maybe I should drive. I mean, I don't expect you slept much last night and we have a long trip ahead of us."

"I'm fine," said Helen emphatically. "Now go get in your side."

As Helen pulled herself up into the driver's seat, her foot slipped. She grabbed the steering wheel at the last second and wrangled her way into the seat.

"You OK, ma'am?" asked the man holding the door.

"Of course, I'm OK!" Helen snapped. "Why wouldn't I be?" Helen could feel her cheeks redden. Could this man tell she had been stoned the night before? Helen put the car in Drive and eased out into the Denver traffic. "Buckle up, Alice! Omaha, here we come!"

CHAPTER 44

ALICE

After fighting their way through the Denver traffic, Alice and Helen finally hit the interstate, a divided band of pavement stretching straight ahead as far as the eye could see. The Rockies had given way to the plains, a vast flat landscape with an impossibly blue sky swept clean by wind and saturated by sun.

Alice settled into her enormous leather seat and took it all in. Every direction revealed a seemingly endless expanse of brown rocky dirt and prairie grass. The small towns resembled sepia–toned postcards from the past. It was easy to imagine a line of covered wagons following the trail on their way to Oregon, grateful for the flat, if barren plains before they had to face the Rockies. Helen had set the cruise control at just over 85 as they swished along the interstate, their primary company gigantic tractor–trailers doing the long haul. Occasionally, a train whistle pulled them out of their reverie.

Neither Helen nor Alice noticed as they sped across the border from Colorado into Nebraska. In such wide–open country, borders seemed meaningless and the highway just an arbitrary stripe of asphalt painted in a straight line across an empty canvas. Now this was a real road trip!

"Uh–oh." Helen sat up a little straighter as she peered in the rearview mirror. A police car was rapidly approaching, lights flashing, siren screaming.

Alice turned her head, startled out of her prairie meditation. "You better pull over, Helen. How fast were you going?"

"Not that fast." Helen slowly braked the mammoth vehicle, flicked on her right–turn signal and pulled onto the shoulder of the highway. She fumbled in her bag for her license while Alice got the rental documents out of the glove compartment. Glancing out the back, Alice saw a solidly built, crew–cut state trooper with a Smokey the Bear hat approaching the car, a large German shepherd in tow.

Helen rolled down the window. "Can I help you, Officer?"

As the trooper started to answer, the dog began barking wildly, lunging toward Helen's open window. The trooper examined the vehicle more critically, taking in the tinted windows, the out–of–state license plate.

"Yes, ma'am. Let's start by you giving me your license and registration. And please, both of you, keep your hands where I can see them."

Helen and Alice handed the papers through the window. Alice turned to Helen with a quizzical look.

"You ladies stay right where you are while I go check these out."

The officer walked back to the shiny black patrol car and got in, presumably to enter some information into his computer. The dog followed reluctantly, casting mournful, disappointed looks at Helen over its shoulder.

"Don't worry, Helen," said Alice, trying to sound reassuring. "I'm sure we'll just get a speeding ticket and be on our way."

"I know. But this is stupid. There are hardly any cars on the road, and I've barely been keeping up with the trucks."

More like passing every one of them, thought Alice. She decided she'd best keep that insight to herself.

A few minutes later, the trooper returned, handing the license and papers back through the window. "I'm afraid I have to ask you ladies to step out of the car. Just leave everything in the car and both of you come to the driver's side."

"There must be some mistake here, officer." Helen was clearly agitated.

"Just do what the man says, Helen. It's probably part of the routine around here."

Helen harrumphed herself out of the car, while Alice climbed out and walked around.

"Do either of you ladies have a weapon?"

"No," they answered in unison, wide–eyed.

"Any illegal drugs?"

"No!" said Helen vehemently. "This is harassment, plain and simple!"

"I'm afraid not. This car has been stopped before and found to be transporting drugs."

"But this is a rental car," Helen explained with exasperation. "We don't control who rented it before us or what they did!"

The officer whistled, and the dog shot out of the car and made a beeline for Helen. Alice started to get nervous.

"You want to reconsider that answer, ma'am?"

"No!" Helen replied indignantly.

"Well, then empty your pockets. You can put everything on the hood of the car."

"This is outrageous! I know my rights. Do you? Or did they forget to teach you that out here in Smokey the Bear country?"

"Helen!" Alice said warningly.

Alice and Helen began emptying their pockets. As Alice was digging deeper, she heard Helen suddenly gasp. There was Helen holding a clear cellophane baggie with a couple dozen gummies in it.

"What the heck, Helen!"

"I just forgot. I bought these the other morning in one of the stores while you were busy talking about flower quality. I thought some of our customers might like them."

"Customers?" The officer studied them more intently, his interest piqued. "You sell cannabis?"

"Well, not yet. We're just getting started. Surely you can understand this isn't for me!"

"Not for you?"

"No!

"Shut up, Helen!" Alice hissed. She was apoplectic.

The officer took the radio mic from his shoulder, pressed his thumb down and began speaking. "This is Trooper 54. Assistance requested. We've got a couple of live ones. I–80, about 2 miles west of Buffalo Springs, heading east. Make sure you send someone who can drive this big–ass SUV of theirs."

Helen, turned to face the open prairie, was close to tears, while Alice's eyes bored two red–hot holes through the back of her head. "Helen, how could you have been so stupid? And for God's sake, be quiet!" Alice whispered. She was beyond angry.

Helen handed the keys to the officer who escorted them a little more roughly than was called for back to the patrol car and into the back seat. Luckily, the exultant dog was locked in a cage behind them.

"OK, la–dees. Welcome to Nebraska!"

CHAPTER 45

HELEN

SEVERAL HOURS LATER AFTER THEIR booking was finished, Helen and Alice followed two guards through a series of heavy metal doors into the belly of the small county jail. Helen was still miffed at the terrible picture they had taken of her and annoyed they had refused to take a second. Alice had glared at the camera, looking every bit the hardened criminal.

As they passed into the women's section of the jail, Helen stared aghast at the cells and the sullen, unkempt collection of women waiting in them. They stopped at an empty cell near the end of the row, and one of the guards pointed to the door and rather impolitely said, "Here ya go." Helen gaped at the 10 x 10 room with its two metal beds, two metal desks, sink and toilet, all welded to the floor. Helen wasn't having it.

"Officer, this simply won't do. I want a single. I mean, I think I have a right to a single."

The guard laughed. "Sorry, lady. We're kinda full tonight and we're just fresh out of singles."

"Maybe she'd like the Presidential Suite," the other guard piped in.

Helen was annoyed. "OK, OK. What about our phone calls?"

"We'll see about that once you get settled." As the two men walked away, a female guard approached and handed them each an orange jumpsuit, instructing them to leave nothing on of their own clothing but their underpants and shoes and to hand over everything else when they were done.

"Oh no, you don't. I'm not taking off my bra." Helen was indignant.

"Oh yes you are, sweetie. I seen some pretty sick stuff done with bras."

"But where do I change?"

"Right here. Do you want me to turn my back?" The guard couldn't help but snicker.

Helen stared at Alice in dismay. *This will be the first and last time we ever dress alike*, she thought. "Don't look," she instructed as she walked into the cell and turned her back to Alice.

"Don't worry," Alice replied tartly as she walked to another corner of the cell.

Now fully clad in their matching orange jumpsuits, they each sat on a bed, chins on fists, fuming. After what seemed like hours, a guard finally appeared. "Up and at 'em, ladies. Let's go make your calls." Both women were on their feet in seconds, determined to be the first out the door.

"I'm calling Dan," said Helen. "You said he was a lawyer. He'll know what to do. Can you give me his number?"

"What? You're calling Dan? You wouldn't even speak to him! And he's my friend. Don't you have anyone else to call?"

"Well, we need a lawyer and you've got to call Bear, right?"

Alice hesitated. "I don't know. I guess I should call Bear, but I really don't want to worry him."

"Of course you should call him! He's your son! And he's got to coordinate getting us out of here."

"Well, I don't see you rushing to call Kim."

Helen glanced up, giving Alice a pointed look. "You need to tell Bear to call Matt right away—and to call Dan. Be sure to tell Bear how to reach him—got it?"

Alice reluctantly gave Helen Dan's number. Helen picked up the phone and began dialing.

"Don't forget to tell him you're with me, Helen."

Helen nodded impatiently.

CHAPTER 46

BEAR

BEAR STEERED HIS TRUCK ONTO the dirt road leading to Jed and Chrissie's just as the sun was setting. As he pulled up next to the barn and put the truck in Park, Rose unbuckled her seatbelt, leaned over and held his face with its newly trimmed beard in her two palms. She smiled, then gave him a soft kiss on the lips.

"Not that I'm complainin', but what was that for, Rose?"

"Nothing in particular. It's just been a great week. We've made good progress on the store, and I have to admit, it's been awfully nice having you all to myself for a few days."

"Amen to that. I'll be happy to see Ma and Helen, but I've loved it being just the two of us." Bear gave Rose a quick kiss back. "Now let's go eat! You got the flowers and wine?"

"Right here, Bear."

Bear and Rose climbed out of the truck and headed toward the farmhouse. The gravelly, melancholy voice of John Prine carried through the screen door and a bright light in the kitchen backlit Chrissie tossing a salad in a wooden bowl on the counter while Jed stirred a pot on the stove. As Bear and Rose walked through the door, Jed and Chrissie looked up, smiling.

"Hey strangers! Welcome!" cried Jed, continuing to stir the pot.

Chrissie dropped the salad utensils and rushed over the give them each a hug and relieve them of the flowers and wine. "We've got so much news for you, you're not going to believe it."

"Good news, I hope," said Bear.

"All good. Just give us a minute to get this on the table, and then we'll fill you in."

In no time, they were all settled at the table with plates of beef stew, home–made biscuits and salad in front of them.

Jed raised his glass of wine. "First, a toast to Bear. We're so excited about the direction our lives are taking and none of it would be happening if it weren't for you and Safe Access."

Everyone raised a glass and happily drank. Rose noticed that Chrissie was drinking water.

"So, what's the big news, Jed?" asked Bear, setting his glass back down on the table.

"You know the Green Zone group has been close to getting licensed by the state, but our biggest hurdle has been securing sufficient start–up capital. Well, yesterday we got word from a bank in New York that we have an anonymous investor who has given us a line of credit we can draw upon up to $500,000! The only stipulation is that he or she, whoever it is, wants us to set up the growing operation in as environmentally responsible a way as possible, even if it costs more."

Bear's and Rose's mouths dropped open. "You're kidding," Bear finally said.

"Nope." Jed and Chrissie were beaming.

"Do you have any idea who it is?" asked Rose.

"None at all," replied Chrissie.

"Are you worried this might not be all on the up–and–up? That this might be a criminal enterprise of some sort?" asked Bear.

"Yeah, we're a little worried. But the bank is a well–known Wall Street investment bank. All they've said is that the funds are coming out of a trust they've administered for years for a very wealthy individual with ties to this area and an interest in seeing Green Zone succeed. We're gonna talk to our lawyer to make sure she thinks everything's OK, and we have a bunch of papers the bank has prepared that she'll have to review."

"This is incredible. I feel like we've just cleared the last major hurdle. Congratulations, guys!" Bear felt like jumping up and down. Everyone traded enthusiastic high–fives. "You said 'so much news.' Not that this isn't enough! But is there more?"

"Two more pieces of news, actually. One involves a weird thing that happened the other day." Bear and Rose looked at Jed expectantly as they continued eating. "Marty came by."

Bear raised his eyebrows, a tiny shiver of panic pulsing through his body. "What did he want?"

"He was nice as can be. Acted like we'd never been anything but the best of buddies. Even wanted to know how you're doin', Bear. Claimed he was acting as a 'broker' for some large dealers and a processor who were lookin' to buy any 'excess' crop from the local growers. As I understand it, a lot of legal growers grow more than they report and sell the excess to people like Marty. The advantage to the farmers is that they can make a lot more money from the illegal weed since they pay no tax. And there's still a market for the cheaper illegal weed."

Rose nodded. "I know a lot of the farmers in Colorado had side deals. It was pretty easy to fly under the radar, and it boosted their profits enough to make it worthwhile."

Bear ran his fingers through his hair, a worried frown creasing his forehead. "I've heard about it, too. But it raises so many questions, I hardly know where to start. What did you tell him, Jed?"

Jed looked at Chrissie. "I said no." Chrissie nodded. "And that was even before we got our anonymous investor! All the families in the co–op talked about it, and we don't want the risk. The licensing process and all the regulations and taxes are a huge pain in the ass, but if we can't make a go of it legally, then we're outta here."

"How did Marty take that?"

"Surprisingly well. I don't think he'll have too much trouble finding some takers, so he didn't seem to feel like he needed to pressure us at all. It'd be interesting to know how he's ended up where he has and who he's working with, but I sure wasn't gonna ask. I couldn't believe it was such an easy conversation."

"Well, I'll be damned," said Bear. "I am so relieved."

"And what about news alert #3?" asked Rose as she smiled at Chrissie.

Chrissie laughed. "What is it about women and men? The women always seem to notice, while the men are clueless."

"What in the world are you two talking about?" Bear was clearly confused.

"We're pregnant," said Chrissie, grabbing Jed's hand.

"Woo–hoo! You saved the best news for last! Congratulations!" Bear got up to give Jed and Chrissie hugs. "But how did you know, Rose?"

"Ah, that's my little secret." Rose and Chrissie laughed.

Bear and Rose held hands under the table as they finished dinner and Jed and Chrissie regaled them with Caleb's latest misadventures. A seemingly intrepid outdoorsman, two–year–old Caleb was climbing everything in sight and bringing Chrissie an endless string of "presents" ranging from spiders to newts to, most recently, a small garter snake. Chrissie told Bear and Rose she was ready for a baby girl and that, after researching all the old wives' tales, she was eating chocolate morning, noon, and night!

The meal over, Jed, Bear and Rose passed a pipe around while Chrissie drank hot chocolate. The perfect mood was suddenly interrupted by the buzzing of Bear's phone. He thought about ignoring it, but then decided he should at least see who was calling. Ma! Now, what could she be calling about?

Bear straightened up, holding the phone in his hand so everyone could see. "So sorry, guys, gotta take this."

Bear hefted himself out of his chair and walked out onto the front porch. "Ma, what's up?" He paused to listen. "What?!? You're in jail?!"

Rose, Chrissie, and Jed, who were straining to listen from the living room, traded shocked looks.

"Don't worry, Ma. I'll get hold of Matt right away. I'm sure he'll know what to do and if he doesn't, he'll know who to call.... OK, OK. I'll call this Dan guy right away, too. I don't understand, though, Ma. Why would they be holding you in jail for possession of a few gummies? ... Oh great.... Don't worry, I'll talk to Matt and Dan, and we'll get somebody there first thing tomorrow. Can you give me Dan's number? ... And yeah, I'll call Aunt Nell and tell her you're not gonna make it.... No, I won't tell her you're in jail if you don't want me to.... OK.... Try to get some sleep if you can, Ma.... I love you, too."

Bear walked back into the house and threw his hands up in the air. "Well, I guess you all heard. Ma and Helen got themselves thrown in jail in someplace called Buffalo Springs, Nebraska. Apparently, Helen got stopped for speeding and forgot she had some gummies in a bag in her pocket. Cannabis isn't legal in Nebraska. But even so, it wouldn't have been a big deal, except Helen said something about the gummies and customers. So now they're charging them with possession with intent to distribute!"

"Oh, God, Bear. I'm so sorry." Rose got up and put her arms around him.

Jed rubbed his forehead. "I'm still confused. Helen had gummies in her pocket?"

"Yeah, I know. Pretty weird. Anyway, let's keep this among ourselves for now. I gotta go call Matt and some guy named Dan. I sure hope this guy Dan knows what to do."

"Keep us posted, Bear," said Chrissie.

After quick hugs all around, Bear linked his arm through Rose's, and they set out into the night. Bear punched Matt's number into his phone as their boots crunched on the gravel in the drive.

CHAPTER 47

ALICE

AFTER RETURNING TO THEIR CELL, Helen turned to Alice. "Which bed do you want?"

"Which *bed* do I want? I don't want either of these beds. I want my bed, or a bed at Aunt Nell's, or even my bed at that fancy–pants hotel of yours!"

"You don't have to get all huffy, Alice."

"Oh, yes, I do. We are in *jail,* Helen, thanks to you!"

"It's not like I meant for this to happen."

"In case you missed this, ignorance is no defense under the law. And this was beyond ignorant, Helen. I have never been in jail, and I don't *want* to be in jail!"

"Well, I've never been in jail, either. You think I want this?! How am I ever going to explain this to Kim?"

"Who gives a shit how you're going to explain this to Kim, Helen?"

"That's about it, Alice!"

"Hey, ladies, pipe down in there!"

Alice stomped over to one of the beds, attempted to plump the cheap foam pillow, and lay down on the hard narrow mattress, her face to the wall.

Alice was furious with Helen. And with herself. How had she gotten herself into this mess? It wasn't like she and Helen were actual friends. Hell, they had barely spoken to each other most of their lives. As she examined her anger, Alice realized that it stemmed from much more than this awful incident. It had been building up for months. Insult by insult. Helen treated Alice like she was somehow inferior in every way. And now look where they were!

Alice felt her blood pressure rising. She had to calm down. All she needed now was to have a heart attack or a stroke in this God–forsaken jail. OK. She'd meditate. That was the answer. Alice tried clearing her mind. She began a body scan, focusing on her forehead, her eyelids, her tongue, her jaw. Nope. She whispered her old secret mantra to herself repeatedly, trying to picture herself in a room with the Maharishi practicing transcendental meditation. She slowed her breathing, inhaling and exhaling deeply. Nothing worked! Alice just stared at the wall.

CHAPTER 48

HELEN

"Rise and shine, ladies!" Helen could hear groans emanating down the length of the cell block as the women began to stir. She'd almost forgotten they weren't in here by themselves.

"What time is it?" croaked Helen, as a guard approached their cell. God, the inside of her mouth felt like it was coated with dirty fake fur.

"Six a.m.! It's your big day, ladies. You've got yourselves an appointment with the Right Honorable Judge Yates at 9:30 a.m., and I hear y'all have a visitor expected this morning."

"But why are you waking us at 6 if our appointment isn't until 9:30? And when is breakfast? I sure could use a cup of strong coffee." Helen looked pleadingly at the short, heavy–set guard, noting the large nightstick hanging from a loop on her belt.

"Ain't no hotel. Breakfast comes when breakfast comes. Hope you like the eggs benedict."

"Ha ha," replied Helen, annoyance edging her voice. "I know you're kidding and it's not very funny."

God, I must look a fright, thought Helen, as she ran her fingers through her hair, trying to bring some order to the unsightly mess. And her face! Why, she hadn't even been able to properly remove her make–up and cleanse her face last night.

Helen turned to look at Alice. Oh, great. Alice was still turned toward the wall, giving the impression of a bright orange beached whale.

"Alice, are you awake?" asked Helen tentatively.

"What do you think? I'm just lying here waiting for my eggs benedict."

"Well, you don't have to be so snippy." Didn't Alice realize this was awful for both of them? And how was Helen supposed to know a few gummies in her pocket would land them in jail?!

Helen got up and began her morning routine of stretches and bends. As she finished, the guard returned with two trays carrying watery oatmeal, dry toast, and tepid coffee that tasted like it had been brewed several days ago. Alice reluctantly turned and sat up, and the two women ate in stony silence, studiously avoiding looking at each other.

As they finished eating, a guard approached and told them their lawyer was ready to talk. The guard unlocked the door and led the two women to a small windowed room with a table and chairs, again all bolted into the floor. Fortunately, the room was approached from their end of the hallway, sparing them another perp walk past their neighbors.

"Dan! Thank God you're here!" Alice gave him a quick hug.

Helen checked out Dan's expensive suit, tie, and shoes. *Whew! Maybe this guy was all right after all.*

"Good to see you both, ladies. I'm so glad you called me. I talked with Matt and Bear last night. They seem like nice guys, and they were sure anxious to get you out of here. We decided it made the most sense for me to handle this. Anyway, I got here as soon as I could. Luckily, I'm admitted in Nebraska, as well as Colorado, and I've been down this path before. So, tell me what happened."

Helen and Alice both began talking at once, the volume rising as they each sought to drown the other out.

"Whoa there. One at a time! Alice, why don't you go first and, Helen, you can fill in anything Alice misses."

After listening to their tale, Dan rubbed his chin. "Well, this sure seems like some kind of misunderstanding to me." Helen and Alice both audibly sighed. "Some kind of over–reaction. Possession of less than an ounce of cannabis—an ounce is a hell of a lot more than 15 or 20 gummies—is a misdemeanor punishable by a fine. And it seems clear you had no intent to sell or distribute within the meaning of the criminal statute. You've got a bail hearing in about an hour and, although it's a little unusual, I'm going to see if we can get the intent to distribute charge dropped. Then you'll pay a fine, and we'll get you on your way."

"Oh, Dan, that would be wonderful." Helen gave Dan her most sincere smile. Helen caught Alice frowning, but plunged ahead anyway. "So who does the talking?"

"I'll do most of the talking." Helen and Alice looked relieved. "But just in case you're asked, let's go over your answer, Helen, about why you had the gummies and what you intended to do with them."

Helen sat up primly, hands folded in front of her. Alice put her head down on the table.

CHAPTER 49

ALICE

THE COURT PROCEEDING WENT OFF without a hitch. Money was wired, and Alice, Helen, and Dan soon stood on the sidewalk in front of the jail.

"Dan, we can't thank you enough," Helen gushed. "And please send us your bill."

"No bill this time—but you two better stay out of trouble." Dan grinned. "It's been a real trip meeting you!"

Dan shook hands with Helen and then turned to Alice. He took both her small soft hands in his large, roughened hands. "Alice, I've enjoyed our time together. You're a special lady. Let's keep in touch."

Alice gave Dan a hug. "I can't thank you enough. You have an open invitation to visit Poplar Point any time you want! It's not as beautiful as Denver, but I'd love to show you around." Alice turned and followed Helen, who had already set off for the car.

Alice and Helen climbed into the Navigator, fastened their seatbelts, and took off for the airport. They were still hours away and they were both anxious to get home. Hopefully, there would be another time for Aunt Nell, thought Alice.

Helen drove excessively cautiously, cars whizzing by her as she intentionally kept the speedometer fixed at five miles below the speed limit. Alice said nothing, although her blood was beginning to boil again as she thought back over what a terrible experience this had been. And what would they have done without Dan, the man Helen had refused to even have dinner with?

As they finally pulled into the lot at the car rental center and parked, Alice turned to Helen. "Helen, I think we need a little break. I'll see you back in Poplar Point." And with that, Alice climbed out of the car, retrieved her backpack, and headed into the terminal, leaving Helen to deal with her three suitcases and whatever other problems she might encounter.

Alice walked hurriedly through the garage and into the crowded terminal. She quickly changed her ticket, choosing a seat in the last row of the plane where she was sure she would never see Helen. After calling Bear one last time to make sure he would be on time picking her up, Alice walked through the shopping area, keeping an eye out for Helen. Got her! There she was at the Gucci counter. Alice headed the other way.

Alice heard them call the flight, but delayed going to the gate, timing her arrival so that she would be one of the last passengers boarding the plane. As she navigated her way down the narrow aisle, she spied Helen in row 7, headphones on, full focus on the Kindle in her lap.

Alice awkwardly settled into the middle seat in the back row, studiously avoiding any eye contact with the passengers on either side of her. She felt bad about being so unfriendly, but she was exhausted. And she was feeling a little guilty about her treatment of Helen. It was unlike her to stay angry for this long, and she knew Helen hadn't done anything on purpose. But it had been a horrible experience. Alice shuddered at the memory, then took the magazine out of the seat pocket. Within two minutes, she was asleep.

CHAPTER 50

ALICE

"MA! MA!" BEAR WAVED AT his mom as she made her way out of the crowded, grungy terminal at Logan to the Arrivals area. "Over here!"

With relief, Alice stepped up her pace and headed toward Bear's truck. She couldn't remember when she had been this happy to see him! She threw her arms around him. "I'm so glad to be back."

Bear hugged her back, then asked, "Where's Helen?"

"I don't know, and I don't care."

Bear pushed Alice to arms–length and looked at her face. "What's going on?"

"I need a break. It was kind of a hard trip."

"Well, it sounded like everything was going OK until your little brush with the law in Nebraska."

"Not my brush with the law. And it didn't feel little. Come on, let's go."

Once home, Alice headed straight to the bathroom for a long tub soak. She lit her lavender candles and tossed a CBD bath bomb into the steaming water. An hour later, she emerged, wrapped in her most comfortable old robe and feeling a lot more like herself. Bear was waiting for her at the kitchen table where he was reading through some catalogues he'd picked up that afternoon.

"You doin' better, Ma?"

"Much." Alice poured herself a cup of tea and sat down at the table across from Bear.

"Anything you want to talk about?"

"Well, as I'm sure you've gathered, things didn't go so well with Helen and me. To be fair, we started off OK, even spent a night getting high."

Bear's eyebrows shot up.

"But these last two days have been terrible. I tried to warn you, Bear. I'm not sure it's possible for the two of us to work together."

"It's a little late for that, Ma. It's not just about you and me and Helen anymore. There's a lot of people depending on us. The farmers in the county who are preparing to start up their cannabis cultivation, Rose and Matt who've been working day and night while you've been gone, all the people who've helped us come this far."

Alice turned to the window and practiced slowing her breathing—in, out, in, out. She tried to reclaim a spirit of generosity, but try as she might, that well had gone dry. "I'm so sorry, honey, but I just don't think I can do this. Of course I want you to continue. I will still be a financial partner, but I'm so tired of Helen. I can't work on the store anymore—at least for a while."

"OK. Take a little time, Ma. It's too soon after the trip for you to make a big decision like this. You'll probably see things differently in a few days."

Alice shook her head. "It's not only the jail experience, Bear. I warned you at the very beginning. Helen and I are too different, and I don't want to spend my days stressed out and unhappy. I've tried, Bear. I've really tried. But this isn't for me."

Bear stood up, clearly upset. "You need to give this some more thought, Ma, before you make any final decision. I'm not going to make you do anything you really don't want to do. But we need to talk some more about this. How about if we plan on getting together tomorrow?" Bear headed for the door.

"What? Can't you stay here tonight?"

"I can't, Ma. I promised Rose I'd be back." Bear walked back and gave his mom a hug. Then he hurried out to his truck as Alice stood at the door watching him leave.

CHAPTER 51

HELEN

HELEN SAT ON KIM'S FRONT porch, her suitcases piled beside her, anxiously waiting for Kim to get home with the key. At long last, Kim pulled into the driveway. One look at Kim's face said it all—she knew.

The kids tumbled out of the backseat, grabbed their backpacks, and ran toward Helen. "Grandma, you're home!" At least someone was glad to see her.

She gave them each a quick hug, her eyes remaining on Kim, who was putting some loose papers in her briefcase and then stepping out of the car. The car door closed with a little extra thump.

"OK, kids, go on in the house and wash up. I need to talk to Grandma for a minute.

"Do you want to tell me what happened, Mom?" Kim managed to give the impression of being both angry and disappointed in her.

"Not really. Let's just say I made a couple of mistakes, and things didn't go too well. But it's all over now."

Kim took in her mother's rumpled appearance and exhausted face. Even her usually perfectly coiffed hair was a mess.

"I'm having a hard time understanding what's going on with you, Mom. I know the break-up of a marriage's painful. But you've gone totally off the deep end. Frankly, it's embarrassing to hear people talking at school about how my mother's been in jail."

"Embarrassing for you?" Helen wasn't entirely surprised, but she was still hurt. "This entire experience was terrible for me. And it was all a huge mistake. They never should have put us in jail."

Kim put her hands on her hips and stared her mom down. "Why don't you just drop this whole insane idea? It's not too late."

Helen paused, thinking. A little surprised at herself, she raised her head and looked Kim straight in the eyes. "I don't think I want to. You are right. I am not a marijuana person. I tried a gummy so I would know what it's like, but now I know, and I really don't need to do that again. But I like the idea of doing something different—something unexpected. I can't go back to my former life. In fact, now that I think about it, I realize I don't want to. I'm tired of my old self. I need to stretch myself."

Kim stared at Helen and shook her head. "Mom, I have no idea what you're talking about. The only thing I can figure is that this must be some weird delayed midlife crisis."

Wow, thought Helen. There were sure a lot of insults packed into that one. "That's OK, Kim. I understand this all seems weird to you; it feels weird to me, too. And maybe it is a late midlife crisis. But things change, people change. And we can't always control everything. It's scary and upsetting, but it can also be good. If we stop growing as people, we might as well pack it in."

In a perfect imitation of her teenage self, Kim rolled her eyes and scoffed. She wasn't buying it.

Helen hesitated, then continued. "Look, Kim. I understand you're upset with me. I truly am sorry. I also know I've been staying with you a lot longer than either of us expected. I don't want to be a burden. We've never finished talking about when I should find my own place.

Kim stiffened. "This is not the time for this discussion, Mom. With Kevin gone, I need you here to cover the gaps when the babysitter's off. At least until I can figure something else out."

Helen was a little surprised, but relieved she didn't need to find a new place right away. Besides, it was nice to know someone needed her—at least temporarily.

"OK, Kim. We can talk about it later. Can you help me get into the house? You can't believe how tired I am."

As they walked into the hallway, Kim abruptly stopped. "Why did Alice and Bear just leave you on the porch, Mom?"

CHAPTER 52

ALICE

Alice woke up the next morning and stretched luxuriously before pushing her feet into her slippers and pulling on her old robe. She was so glad to be home. What a relief to have slept in her own bed, with her own pillow. Even her CPAP had felt like a welcoming friend. And while they had been out West, spring had sprung in Poplar Point. The sound of robins singing filled the air.

Alice dressed quickly and drove into town for one of Millie's chocolate croissants and a cup of coffee.

Must be my lucky day, thought Alice, as she pulled into a parking space right in front of Millie's. But as she walked into the café, a bad vibe hit her. Something had happened; she was sure of it.

Alice gave Millie her "come see me when you can" look and took a seat at her usual spot near the window. The café was busy, but unusually quiet. A few minutes later, Millie came to the table and bent over to give Alice a quick hug and a kiss. "Heard you ran into a bit of trouble in Nebraska, honey." Millie smiled.

Oh boy, here we go. How in the world had Millie heard about it already? Then again, Poplar Point was a small town, and while it might be struggling, its gossip mill was always running at maximum capacity.

"So, what's going on, Millie?"

"You haven't heard? Faye Larson died a couple of nights ago. No foul play. Apparently, she just had a heart attack. Poor Brendan came home late from some meeting at the church, and she had already passed."

Alice gasped. "Oh, no. That's terrible."

"Listen, I'm a bit short–handed today. Let me grab you a cup of coffee and then I'll be back as soon as I can." Millie rushed away, waving to the next set of customers coming in the door.

Alice stared at the table, her shoulders slumped. Poor Faye. Home alone like that, with no one to help her. Memories of Arlo's heart attack came flooding back. As terrible as it had been, Alice was so grateful she had been there to hold Arlo and call for help. Alice hoped that when her time came, she wouldn't be alone.

Alice reflected on her recent conversations with Faye. What was all that crazy talk about exit signs about? And the warnings about Brendan? Faye certainly had had some problems. Everyone knew that. But still Alice felt so sad. Why had she let Faye just walk off without making sure she was all right?

Alice considered how little she truly knew about Faye. They had lived in the same small town most of their lives and yet Alice couldn't recall any recent conversation she had had with Faye about how her life was going or how she was feeling. Poor Brendan, too. Alice couldn't think of a single close friend he had. Except Willow? Alice felt sick.

Millie set a cup of coffee on the table and collapsed into a seat. "I've only got a minute, but I just have to hear how you are."

"I feel so bad, Millie. Poor Brendan. Poor Faye. I came in today feeling sorry for myself and now I wish I had taken the time—even just once—to reach out to Faye." Millie nodded, placing her warm hand on Alice's.

Millie rose. "I'm afraid I better get back to it. We've been crazy busy ever since Rose left." Noting the guilty look on Alice's face, Millie rushed to say, "Don't worry. It's not your fault. I had never intended to hire Rose permanently, and I am so happy that she has found a place with you and Bear. She and Bear seem so happy."

"That they do. I hardly even see Bear these days," mused Alice. "Any news on that ex–husband of Rose's?"

"Thankfully, not a word. It's been months now and Rose has calmed down. She's an incredibly strong woman. The divorce is moving forward, and we're all just hoping he has decided to let her be." Millie gave Alice an affectionate hug and headed back to the busy counter. "I'll see you at the funeral if not before, Alice."

Alice drove home and spent the afternoon doing laundry and restocking the pantry. Just as the sun was setting, she heard Bear's truck pull into the drive. Perfect! She positioned herself at the kitchen table and waited for Bear to walk in.

"Hey, Ma. You're looking better!" Bear headed straight to the refrigerator and grabbed a cold beer.

"Yup. I feel better, too. So, how's everything going with Rose?"

Bear laughed as he pulled out a chair. "You sure don't waste time getting to the point. She's awesome, Ma. And she really likes you."

"Well, that's good. I just want you to know that I'm happy for you, Bear."

"Where'd that come from?"

"Faye Larson's death hit me hard, and I've been thinking about the importance of family and friends. I'm so glad you've found Rose."

"Me, too. Have you given any more thought to the store, Ma? I saw Helen moping around town this afternoon. You two gotta get this straightened out."

"I know. I've been thinking about it. I'm just not sure what I want to do. By the way, remember Dan, the lawyer who helped Helen and me out in Nebraska?"

"Sure do. Seemed like a nice enough fella."

"Well, turns out he's been doing some work in Boston and he's coming back into town for a meeting in the next few days. I've invited him to visit for the weekend."

Bear looked shocked. "Visit here?"

"Don't get the wrong idea, honey. I am not lookin' to replace your dad. But I sure could use some new friends, and I thought maybe Dan could give me some advice. Rose might want to talk to him, too."

"Ohhh–kay." Bear still looked troubled. "But be careful what you get yourself into, Ma. You're an awfully trusting person."

Alice burst out laughing. "Do you believe this? You telling me to be careful?"

CHAPTER 53

HELEN

HELEN SAT ON THE FLOOR in the playroom with Emma and Ben, trying to muster some interest in the 500–piece jigsaw puzzle spread out around them. She had slept in unusually late this morning and then taken a short walk around town. She was feeling more like herself now.

Every time she thought about Alice at the airport, though, it was like a knife slicing into her gut. She understood Alice was upset, but the intensity of Alice's anger had taken her aback. She knew she had to talk to Alice, but she was afraid to call her. What if she was still so mad?

"Grandma, you're not looking at the puzzle pieces!" Eight–year–old Emma pouted. "Don't you want to play with us?"

"Of course I do, honey. I just have a lot on my mind."

"You mean like going to jail?" Ben looked at her with a mixture of embarrassment and admiration.

"Where did you hear that, Ben?"

"I heard you and Mom talking. Did you really?"

"I did, Ben, but it was all a misunderstanding. I got to stay there one night, but then they realized they had made a mistake." Might as well make it sound like an adventure, thought Helen. Actually, in a way it was.

"Wow! What was it like?"

"Nothing I ever want to do again. Listen, I'm going to go upstairs for a minute. Why don't you two see if you can finish the puzzle before I get back?" Thankfully, both kids nodded and refocused on the puzzle.

Nothing like a challenge to get them going!

Helen was surprised at how heavy her legs felt as she climbed the stairs to her room. As she reached the second–floor landing, her phone rang. Helen snatched it out of her pocket, hoping it was Alice. Jack! What could he be calling about? By mutual agreement, they had turned everything over to their lawyers.

"Hello," Helen answered somewhat coldly.

"Hi, Helen. How are you doing?"

"I'm fine. What can I do for you?"

"We just haven't talked in a while, and I wanted to be sure you're OK. Been busy?"

"Very busy. Why are you asking?" Helen's bullshit antennae quivered.

Jack scoffed. "I heard you're opening a pot shop. What a joke. Everyone here's laughing about it. And what's this about spending a night in jail?"

Helen had figured this was coming sooner or later, and she had rehearsed a variety of repartees ranging from telling Jack what an incompetent fool he was to how much she had hated being married to him—neither of which was entirely true, but both of which felt damn good. To her surprise, though, now that the moment had come, the hurt and resentment she had been nursing for months seemed to have waned. It wasn't gone, probably never would be, but it wasn't the same all–consuming fire pit of emotion.

"Honestly, Jack, I couldn't care less what the people in Boston are saying. Listen, I'm awfully busy right now. Been nice talking to you."

Helen punched the red button. Well! She was certainly burning bridges right and left these days! Now why had she been coming upstairs? She had no idea. Oh, well. Helen pulled her shoulders back and headed back down the stairs. Time to focus on the important things—like jigsaw puzzles. And making amends with Alice.

CHAPTER 54

ALICE

Friday morning, Alice turned into the church parking lot. She was pleased to see the lot was almost full, a good turn–out for Faye.

Alice stepped out of the car, noting the line of people waiting to enter the church, almost all of them dressed in black. After spending an hour going through her meager wardrobe looking for something appropriate to wear, she had confirmed she didn't own anything even approaching black. She thought back to the small service they had had at the beach for Arlo, the rule of the day being that everyone had to wear something bright, colorful, even flamboyant in celebration of a life well–lived.

Well, to each his own. Alice wasn't judging. She just hoped nobody else was!

Alice joined the back of the line, her long muted blue and green dress adding a touch of color to the otherwise somber scene as she began saying hello to the neighbors and friends standing near her.

Brendan was just inside the church door, greeting people as they arrived. He looked exhausted and somehow deflated. As Alice neared the door, Brendan glanced up and saw her. A frown crossed his face. "Alice, may I speak to you for a moment?"

Alice was surprised he would pull her out of the line, but she obligingly stepped into the church and followed Brendan into a side hallway.

Brendan was livid. "What are you doing here, Alice? You and that worthless son of yours have trampled on everything I believe in, putting your desire for a quick buck and an artificial high above the health and welfare of our children. I'm sure Faye felt the same way. Indeed, if I hadn't been so consumed with trying to save the town these past months, I would have had more time for her. You need to leave."

Stunned, Alice stumbled back toward the wall. She felt like someone had just punched her in the gut. She knew Brendan had been terribly upset by the Town Meeting vote, but she hadn't seen much of him over the past few months. She had no idea he was still so angry or that he held her personally responsible. "I'm sorry, Brendan," she stuttered, fighting back tears. "Of course I'll leave if you don't want me here. I'm terribly sorry about Faye."

Alice backed hastily out of the hallway, turned, and walked outside and down the steps. Curious stares followed her, but Alice kept her eyes straight ahead and tried to appear like nothing out of the ordinary had just happened.

Once she was safely inside the Subaru, the dam broke and the tears flowed. How awful! Brendan's accusations had left her deeply shaken. Had the hope of making money truly lured her into something evil? Had she put her own interests ahead of her community's? Did other people see her the same way Brendan did? And why hadn't she given more thought to Faye's odd outbursts? Had they been a cry for help? But really—how was Faye's death in any way her fault?

Alice drove home. Oh, God, Dan was arriving the next morning. Now she wished she hadn't told him he could come.

CHAPTER 55

ALICE

THE NEXT MORNING, ALICE WAS sitting on the edge of her chair in the living room when at last she heard a car turn into the driveway. She stood and walked nervously toward the door, then stopped.

Get hold of yourself, Alice! You're a grown woman, for Pete's sake, with a mind of your own, not an insecure teenager on her first date.

Alice opened the front door just as Dan walked across the screen porch, small suitcase in hand. She forced herself to smile.

"Dan! Welcome to Poplar Point. Come on in."

Dan walked through the door, put down his bag and gave her a small kiss on the cheek. He looked around. "It's great to see you, Alice. I have to tell you, this is just how I pictured it."

Alice took Dan's jacket and carefully folded it over the back of a chair, then pivoted to face him. "It's great to see you, too, Dan, but I just want to make sure that there's not any misunderstanding here. That I haven't somehow given you the wrong impression. I mean, I think it's important that we get off on the right foot."

Dan looked at her quizzically. Alice could feel her face redden. *Get off on the right foot?? What the hell am I even talking about? Just spit it out, girl.*

"What I mean to say, Dan, is that I'm not looking for sex."

There was an awkward silence. Finally, Dan spoke. "Well, Alice, I didn't think you were. You didn't strike me as the type to hop in bed with someone you barely know. Besides, to be honest with you, I'm not here for sex, either." Dan smiled innocently.

Relief flooded through Alice's veins, as a tiny voice in the back of her brain whispered, "Alice, he doesn't find you attractive." *What the hell? You've got to stop this, Alice!*

"The truth is, I've been lonely since my wife died. And you said you'd been lonely, too. So, I figured two lonely people might as well get together and have some fun for a change. I don't know anyone in the area and I'm stuck on this case in Boston for a while. But if you're not comfortable...."

"Oh, I'm comfortable. I think it's a great idea, Dan!"

"Well, good. Now that we've got that settled, where do I put my stuff?"

Alice led Dan upstairs to Bear's old bedroom where he threw his suitcase on the bed. For the next two hours, Dan and Alice sat the kitchen table, deep in conversation. Alice had told Dan a lot about her life when they had dinner in Denver, but Dan had not talked much about his. Now he revealed himself to be a wonderful storyteller, regaling Alice with tales of his two grown daughters and his three young granddaughters. Alice especially loved his stories of taking his "citified" grandchildren camping and fishing.

"My worst night ever was once when I had two of my granddaughters, Callie and Jenny, camping out in a tent deep in the woods up near Golden. I don't know why I thought this was a good idea. And I have no idea why their parents ever let me take them. They were pretty little at the time—maybe three and five, or something like that."

"Three and five?" Alice laughed. "You're out of your mind, Dan!"

"Anyway, getting everyone to sleep was a terrible ordeal. Callie, the littler one, was particularly unhappy. She didn't like her pillow and missed her mom. I finally got her stuffed into a sleeping bag with her older sister, and everyone went to sleep. Then, in the middle of the night, I startled awake to Jenny shaking me and crying, saying she couldn't find Callie. I dragged myself out of my sleeping bag and, sure enough, Callie was gone. Panic set in as I imagined myself calling Callie's mom to tell her I'd lost her three–year–old daughter in the Rockies. Jenny and I searched the tent frantically and then just as I was about to leave the tent, Jenny screamed that there was a baby monster. Heart flip–flopping in my chest, I whirled around and, sure enough, I spotted the teensiest movement at the very bottom of Jenny's sleeping bag. I unzipped it all the way, looked in and there was Callie—curled up in a tiny ball at the bottom of the bag, still fast asleep. I almost cried I was so relieved. I swore the girls to secrecy and I've never shared 'our little secret' with anyone until now. Damn near gave me a heart attack."

Alice was laughing so hard her stomach hurt.

That evening, Alice took Dan to Millie's and introduced him around. She got tremendous enjoyment out of all the raised eyebrows. After dinner, they returned to Alice's. Dan was tired from all the traveling and his day–long meeting, so they took turns in the upstairs bathroom, then said good night and went to their separate rooms. Before long, Alice could hear Dan snoring away.

Alice lay in bed missing Arlo. A day never went by that she didn't think of him, but nights were always the worst. For so many years, she had slept with her back curled into Arlo's big body. Sleeping next to Arlo was a bit like sleeping in a ditch with a large heating pad surrounding you, but she'd loved it. She had felt totally safe and protected, secure in the knowledge that Arlo loved her and would always care for her. Then he'd left her.

Sometime in the middle of the night, Alice climbed out of bed and slipped her bathrobe on. She tiptoed out of her room and across the hall, turning the knob on Dan's door as quietly as she could. She eased the door open and then moved to stand by the side of the bed. Dan was deep asleep, his snoring reminiscent of cicadas on a hot summer's night. "Dan," she whispered. Dan woke with a start, startled by the blurry vision of a rounded woman in a fleece bathrobe standing next to the bed.

"Alice! Are you OK?" Dan pulled himself into a sitting position.

"Everything's fine, Dan. I'm just so tired of sleeping alone. Can I just lie next to you for a while?"

Dan was clearly having some trouble processing Alice's request, but ever the gentleman, he nodded his head. "Sure, Alice. Come on in." Dan scooched over against the wall, making as much room for Alice as he could. Alice lay down, her back pressed against Dan's side. Dan could hear her softly crying. He began caressing her hair with his hand.

"Oh, Alice. Now don't you worry. Just lie here and be still. Everything's OK."

Alice wiped her eyes. "I know. I just couldn't sleep. I just hate sleeping by myself."

"Well, now you don't have to. Here now, just close your eyes."

Within minutes, Alice was sound asleep and Dan was the one staring at the ceiling. Truth be told, though, he was glad for the company, even if it wasn't quite all he had hoped for. Having spent his entire adult life living with girls and women, Dan had given up trying to understand them and had instead committed himself to patience. Next time, though, he had to figure out how to get a bigger bed!

CHAPTER 56

HELEN

SUNDAY MORNING, HELEN SAT IN the kitchen at Kim's twiddling her thumbs, waiting for Kim and the kids to return from church and Sunday school. This was crazy. It had now been almost a week since she and Alice had gotten home and they still hadn't spoken to each other. Well, there's no time like the present. Alice was probably sitting at home twiddling her thumbs, too.

Twenty minutes later, Helen pulled into Alice's drive. Mustering her courage, she stepped out of the car and cautiously approached the screen porch. "Alice, Alice! Are you in there?" There was no answer. Helen waited a couple of minutes, then opened the screen door and crossed the porch to the front door. Again, this time accompanied by a knock, she called out. "Alice, are you there?"

Just as she was about to give up, the front door swung open. Helen gasped, almost losing her balance as she hastily stepped back. Her jaw dropped as she took in Dan's tousled hair and loosely knotted bathrobe. "Dan! What are you doing here?"

"Helen, I thought that might be you! How are you? It's great to see you! Come on in!" Dan reached out to usher her in the door, but Helen, still imitating a deer in the headlights, continued backing away.

"Uh, uh, I was just stopping by to see Alice. Is she here?"

"In the shower."

Well, at least *they're* not in the shower, Helen thought, her face reddening. "What are you doing here, Dan?" Helen sputtered.

"Just stopped by for a quick visit. I had a meeting in Boston this past week, so thought I'd check out Poplar Point. I was hoping we'd run into each other. You girls made quite an impression, you know." Dan grinned.

Lord, get me out of here, thought Helen. "Just tell Alice I stopped by. Great to see you, Dan." Mustering as much dignity as she could, Helen turned and walked casually to her car.

Good God, what was I thinking just dropping by? And what is Dan doing here??

CHAPTER 57

ALICE

ALICE STEPPED OUT OF THE upstairs bathroom just in time to hear the screen storm slam and tires spin in the driveway. Good God, that had sounded like Helen's voice!

Alice hurried into her room and threw on some clothes. As she started out the bedroom door, she hesitated. What was she going to say to Dan? *Good morning, Dan! How'd you sleep?* Or *Good Morning Dan! Hope I wasn't too much of a bed hog last night!*

Alice groaned. What had she been thinking? When she woke up this morning in Bear's bed, there was a warm indentation in the bed next to her where she knew Dan had been, but he was gone. What in the world had Dan thought when he woke in the middle of the night to find an older, somewhat plump woman in a flannel nightgown and fleece bathrobe asking if she could get in his bed and just lie next to him? What choice had he had but to say sure? And now here she was, afraid to go downstairs in her own home!

Alice pasted a smile on her face and made her way down the stairs and into the kitchen where she found Dan standing at the kitchen sink in his bathrobe finishing a cup of coffee.

Dan turned his head at her entry, a comfortable grin on his face. "Well, if it isn't the lady of the night!"

"OK, Dan." Alice walked to the cupboard and took down a bowl and a box of cereal. "I know it must have seemed a little strange having me appear like that. I'm awfully sorry if I made you uncomfortable."

"Uncomfortable? Why, Alice, it was wonderful! The best sex I've had in years!"

Alice looked at him, an expression of pure horror on her face. "Sex?" she whispered. "Dan, I don't even remember it!"

Dan looked crestfallen. "You don't remember it?"

Still holding the cereal box in midair, Alice began to stutter, "I… I… I mean… no, I don't." Alice could feel her cheeks turning red.

Suddenly, Dan burst out laughing, the kind of deep belly laugh that is hard to control. He turned and put his hands on Alice's shoulders. "I'm sorry, Alice. Nothing happened—other than you snored a bit, and I stared at the ceiling for a while. I just couldn't help myself. This was too good an opportunity to pass up!" Dan was beaming.

"Dan! That was not funny! You had me worried!" Dan's laughter was contagious and, despite her jumbled emotions of annoyance, embarrassment, and relief, Alice found herself laughing, too. She finished pouring her cereal, added some milk, and collapsed into a chair at the table. Dan sat in the chair next to her, cradling an almost empty cup of coffee.

Her mouth full of Cheerios, Alice mumbled, "Hey, was that Helen I heard at the door?"

"Yup." Dan's eyes twinkled. "I invited her in, but she took off faster than greased lightnin'."

"What'd she want?"

"She was looking for you, Alice, but I told her you were upstairs in the shower."

This time, Alice burst out laughing. "Oh, no, you didn't? Oh, poor Helen. She must have been totally confused."

"Properly scandalized is more like it." Dan paused, taking in a deep breath. "You know, Alice, I've noticed that you change the subject every time Helen comes up. What's going on between you two?" He looked at her kindly. "Of course, you can just tell me to mind my own business, but if you do want to talk about it, I'm all ears."

Alice sighed and rested her elbows on the table. "There's not much to tell. I was so mad at Helen for getting us arrested. Honestly, Dan, if she had just thought before she started spouting off about our marijuana customers, we never would have ended up in jail. When we finally got to the airport, I changed my seat on the flight home and I haven't spoken to her since."

Dan looked mildly surprised.

"I know this may seem like a bit of an over–reaction, but, take my word for it, things have been building up for a long time. Helen is constantly telling me what to do, when to do it, and how to do it. She treats me like I'm an idiot, and then she pulls some stupid shit like this. I've just had it."

Dan sat quietly, waiting for Alice to continue.

"It's true. I've always been a bit hot–tempered. The thing I've loved about mindfulness is how it has helped me learn to explore my emotions, including anger, with compassion and understanding. I think I've gotten a lot better at handling my feelings. But doesn't there come a point where you just have to walk away from something or someone who makes you feel so bad about yourself?"

Dan looked at Alice sympathetically. "That's certainly something to think about, Alice. As far as your Nebraska experience goes, though, do you know how many people get pulled over every year as they cross the border from Colorado with a little marijuana in their pockets? It's the greatest money–making machine for Nebraska since the invention of speed cameras! You and Helen have both been pulled way out of your usual comfort zones at a time when neither of you is feeling your best. And you're both strong women. I'm not surprised it's been a bumpy ride."

Alice's head was bowed. "You're right. I do have to get past this somehow and make up with Helen—for my sake and everyone else's." Alice looked up and smiled. "But I sure wish I'd been here to see the look on her face when you opened the door in your bathrobe!"

CHAPTER 58

BEAR

JUST AS THE SUN WAS beginning to set, sending shoots of pale purple, pink, and orange across the sky, Bear turned into the driveway by his trailer and climbed out of the truck. He was in a great mood. Everything seemed to be progressing on time with the store, the Grow Zone Co–Op was taking off, and he and Rose were getting more serious by the day. The only problem was the latest fallout between his mother and Helen, but Bear was pretty sure they would smooth things over sooner or later. Hell, they'd been here before.

"Hey—you!" Startled, Bear whipped around to find a man striding toward him. Tall and athletic–looking, with thick blond hair and blue eyes, the man seemed tired, tense, and belligerent. Bear took in the dirty jeans and worn leather jacket. He had the sense the man had been traveling for a while.

Before Bear had time to register anything else, the man was on him, delivering a vicious punch to his gut. Bear moved in the nick of time to avoid the man's knee and, breathing hard, backed away.

"Who the fuck are you?" Bear shouted between gasps of breath as he leaned forward, arms wrapped around his middle.

"Where's Rose? I heard you two have something going on, and I'm here to get her."

"Well, she's not here, man." Bear pulled himself upright and raised both hands as though he was about to be arrested, trying to defuse the situation while readying himself for the next attack. "There's nothing going on, and I don't have any idea where she is. What do you want with her?"

The man stood his ground, fists clenched, anger and hostility pouring off of him like rain running down a sidewalk. "That's bullshit. I was told she's got a room in town and that she's usually either here or there. She's not in her room. So I figure she must be here. Tell me where she is."

"And why would I do that?"

"Because she's my wife, and we've got things to settle. I'm not leaving here without her."

Bear took another step back, his eyes squinting and fists bunching. It was like standing in an electric field of rippling tension and violence.

"I've driven all the way from Colorado to find her and you're gonna help me."

"Hey, man. I can't help you. I barely know her, and like I said, I don't know where she is."

"Unlock your trailer."

"Hell, no. Back off, or I'll call the police."

"You got something to hide? You call the police, and I'll know Rose is staying here."

Bear thought quickly. He was sure Rose wasn't here—she had driven into Boston for the day—but if he opened the door, would it be obvious Rose was living here? He had to take the chance. "Fine, fine. Just calm down. I'll let you in, but I'm telling you—Rose is not here, and my girlfriend is gonna be super–pissed if you mess with her stuff." Bear's hand was shaking as he struggled with the key. What if this was a mistake?

As Bear pushed the door open, the man shoved him aside and stepped into the trailer. In less than a minute, he was back outside.

"OK, she's not here. But I'm gonna find her and you better not get in my way." The man stalked back down the drive to the edge of the woods. Bear heard a car engine fire and caught a brief glimpse of a black sports car with the top down tearing down the road, its muffler much in need of repair. *Asshole.*

Hands shaking, Bear grabbed his phone out of his pocket and speed–dialed Rose. No answer. He left a message and sent her a text, then climbed back in his truck.

The store was dark as he crept by, no sign of Rose having returned. Bear raced into town and pulled up in front of Millie's. No light shone in the window of Rose's room above the café. Bear was so upset he never even registered the incredible smells coming from the kitchen as he charged into Millie's. He scanned the café and then peeked in the kitchen. No Rose. After impatiently waiting for Millie to finish with a customer, they both rushed to the kitchen.

"Millie, Rose's husband is here looking for her. He's out of control. I've gotta let her know, but I can't reach her. Do you know where she is? Is she back from Boston yet?"

Millie grabbed Bear's arms. "I'm so upset I can barely function, Bear. He came in here a while ago. I called her the second he left to give her the heads–up, but she didn't answer. I'm sorry, Bear. I should have thought to call you right away. I was just so shaken. Have you tried calling and texting her?"

"Of course. There's no answer." Bear closed his eyes and took a deep breath. "I'm heading over to the police station." Bear paused as he headed toward the door. "You know, I don't even know this asshole's full name. Do you?"

"Tony—uh, Anthony Walsh." As Bear rushed out the door, Millie called behind him. "Please let me know as soon as you get in touch with her."

Patrick Graves was packing up to leave when Bear burst through the front door of the police station. He looked at Bear suspiciously. "Trouble in pot paradise, Bear?"

"No. Do you know Rose Marchetti? She moved here last fall and was working at Millie's. Now she's working with Ma and me on the store."

"Yeah. I've seen her around."

"Some guy in a black convertible was out at my place about 20 minutes ago. He sucker–punched me and made me open my trailer to show him Rose wasn't there. Says he's here to get Rose and threatened me if I didn't help."

"Did you get his name?"

"Yes. Anthony Walsh—from Denver. Rose was married to him, but left. He seems super violent. Out in Denver, Rose had a restraining order against him and she heard a while ago that he'd gotten out of prison. He'd been serving time for an assault on her. I'm real worried, Patrick." Bear was so upset he almost couldn't get the words out.

"You here to press assault charges, Bear?"

"No." Bear wanted to punch him in the face. "I'm not here for myself, Patrick. I'm here for Rose! Can you at least pass the word around to keep an eye out for this dude? I think he could hurt Rose—badly."

"Well, we can't control what kinds of folks pass through town, especially now that we're getting a marijuana store. Sometimes you get what you ask for." Before Bear could respond, Patrick continued. "You say he's driving a black convertible?"

"Yeah, a black sports car with a bad muffler. Should have Colorado plates. Tall, blond, fit and madder than hell."

"OK, Bear. I'll put the word out, and we'll let you know if we see anything." Patrick continued packing up his bag.

And fuck you, too, thought Bear, as he stomped out of the police station.

CHAPTER 59

BEAR

Bear was pacing up and down the length of his trailer, willing himself not to panic, when his phone finally rang.

"Rose! Where are you?"

"On my way back from Boston. I just pulled over and saw the messages from you and Millie." Rose paused. "Bear, I'm so scared." Rose sounded far away.

Bear closed his eyes for a minute. "I know. Tony was super agitated. Yelling that you're his wife and threatening to take you back to Denver. And he knows a lot. I'm worried, too."

A sob caught in Rose's throat. "What am I going to do?"

Bear felt like his heart would burst. "Don't worry, Rose. We'll figure something out. But the first thing we have to do is decide where you're going to stay tonight."

"I guess I could stop at a motel or something and try to get back into the shelter in Boston tomorrow. But, Bear, right now I just want to be with you."

"I know, Rose. Me, too. But we gotta be smart about this." Bear ran his fingers through his hair. "How about if you pick up some food along the way and we stay in the back room at the store tonight? There's even an old mattress in the room. I don't think anyone would think to look for you there."

"I can do that. I even have a sleeping bag in the back of my car. It's come in handy before." Rose gave a short, sad laugh. "Promise you'll stay with me, Bear. I don't want to be alone."

"I promise. I want to be with you, too, Rose."

Bear could hear Rose crying softly. He felt like crying himself. "Oh, Rose, you know I love you, don't you?" Bear took a deep breath. It was a relief to have said it.

"I know. I love you, too." He could hear Rose blowing her nose.

"Oh, Rose." Bear sighed. He wished he could throw his arms around her right now. "We've gotta be super careful getting to the store. Tony's driving a black sports car with a bad muffler. Do you know it?"

"No."

"Keep a close eye out, and if you see him, go straight to the police station."

"OK."

"Call me as soon as you're close. I'll hide the truck and meet you at the store. Don't worry. We'll get through this."

Bear hung up and immediately called the police station. No answer. Great. He hesitated to call 911. Good thing he had Patrick's cell.

"Whadaya want, Bear?" Bear could hear a baseball game on the TV in the background. Patrick sounded annoyed.

"You might be interested to know there's no answer at the police station, Patrick."

"Yeah, well, we're a little short-staffed."

"I wanted to let your guys know that Rose and I will be staying in the back room at the store tonight. I will either be with her or in my truck nearby keeping watch. Can your guys keep an eye out for this Tony guy and be sure to let me know right away if he's spotted? You've got my number, right?"

"We'll try. But I can't promise much, Bear." Patrick hung up.

Bear sat down in his lounger and thought. What did he need for the night? Lots of coffee, that's for sure. And he needed to get his rifle cleaned and ready; it had been some time since he'd been hunting. First, though, he better call his mom.

CHAPTER 60

ROSE

HANDS SHAKING ON THE WHEEL, Rose stared out the windshield at the cars whizzing by. Tears rolled down her cheeks. She had so hoped she was done with Tony. How had he found her? And if he could find her all the way across the country in Poplar Point, he could find her anywhere. She'd hired a lawyer and filed for a divorce. What more could she do? How would this ever end?

After a few minutes of crying, Rose sat up straighter and wiped her face. *Pull yourself together, Rose!* She had faced many challenges in her life — an abusive father, an alcoholic mother, and then Tony. She had always prided herself on being strong, on being able to stand on her own two feet and deal with any problem that came her way. She was a survivor. Now she had a chance at a good life. She had friends. Good friends. And Bear. She would tell him everything—about her life, about Tony, about what he and Poplar Point meant to her. Together, they would figure this out. She would not let Tony ruin it for her, no matter what it took.

Rose put the car back in Drive and cautiously pulled back out onto the highway. Somehow, she would make this work. Other women, lots of women, had faced this—or worse. She just had to get back to Poplar Point—and to Bear.

CHAPTER 61

ALICE

ALICE WAS SITTING AT HOME, despondent. She couldn't work up the energy to eat dinner or even roll a joint. She had enjoyed Dan's visit a lot. He was a good listener and a lot of fun. It had been nice to have a man around again. But now he was gone, and she was alone. All the pain and turmoil of the past week had come rushing back.

She hadn't gotten over Brendan's reaction at the funeral. Sure, she'd been humiliated. But more importantly, she had been deeply hurt. She had never wanted to be the source of pain in anyone's life, particularly Brendan's while he was struggling with the loss of Faye. She was still shocked that Brendan had been so upset with her. They had never been close, but they had known each other all their lives. How could he think she didn't care about the town? And what did she have to do with Faye's death?

And then there was Helen. She'd been so angry about getting arrested and going to jail. And when Dan had told her about Helen stopping by and seeing him in his bathrobe, Alice had laughed, enjoying the image of Helen scurrying back to her car, a shocked look on her face. But she knew that her anger went deeper than that, that it had been building up for a long time. She paused, remembering learning once about the six root "kleshas" in Buddhism, negative emotional states that cause suffering. And of them, anger was one of the worst. What was it the Buddha said about anger? Oh, yes—you are the first victim of your own anger. Alice knew that by continuing to allow her anger to fester, she was hurting herself. She definitely had to call Helen tomorrow.

Alice settled back in her chair and put her feet up on the ottoman. Maybe a short meditation would help.

Sometime later—a few minutes? an hour?—Alice jolted awake as the Eagles' "Take It Easy" began playing on her phone. Why would Bear be calling her now? Still groggy, Alice swiped. "Bear?"

Within seconds, Alice was sitting bolt upright, listening to Bear's description of his run–in with Rose's husband, Tony, and the threats he had made. Alice briefly shut her eyes, imagining what Rose must be feeling right now.

Alice wasn't too comfortable with Bear and Rose's plan to stay in the store overnight, but she couldn't think of a better alternative. Rose could stay with her, but Bear was no doubt right that it was better to have her more out of the way—someplace where Tony would be less likely to spot her or her car.

Bear promised to call if there were any further developments, and Alice hung up. She leaned back in her chair, overcome by exhaustion and despair. I'm so tired, she thought. I need to go upstairs. But instead of dragging herself out of the chair, she sank deeper into the soft cushions. Her eyes closed, and soon she dozed again.

CHAPTER 62

BEAR

An hour later, Bear was standing at the store's back door when he heard Rose's car approaching. Rose passed by the parking lot, turned off her lights, and pulled in behind the shed and dumpster, well out of sight of any passing cars. He walked swiftly to her car, the only illumination the soft light from the moon partially hidden by clouds.

Rose ran to him. "Bear." She buried her head in his chest, hugging him tightly. Bear hugged her back, his chin resting on top of her bent head.

"Don't worry, Rose."

Rose pulled back up and looked up at him, the moonlight reflecting in her moist eyes. "I'm sorry I dragged you into this, Bear, but a part of me is glad he's finally here and we can get this over with. I can't live my whole life with the threat of Tony hanging over me."

Bear gave her a squeeze, then reached into the car for the food bag. They both paused, listened to the silence, then moved together to the store.

Once inside, Bear placed a small candle on the floor, figuring it would give them enough light to eat without attracting attention. He carefully leaned his rifle and flashlight against the wall within easy reach and plugged in both of their cell phones. Neither of them had any appetite, but they forced themselves to share a bottle of water and a dry sandwich from a gas station stop, then curled up together on the mattress.

Time ticked slowly by as they lay in each other's arms, talking softly. Sometime around one, Rose drifted off. With Rose's head resting heavily on his chest, Bear was quiet, listening and thinking. How were they going to convince Tony to leave, that it was all over and he was better off back in Denver?

Suddenly, Bear heard it. The low rumble of a bad muffler. Alert now, Bear slowly extracted his arm from beneath Rose and pushed off the mattress, reaching for his rifle.

He stood stock still, listening. Yes, there it was again. It sounded like Tony was driving back and forth in front of the store. Then all was quiet.

Bear hesitated. Was he better off waiting in the dark storeroom with Rose, hoping Tony had given up and moved on? Or did he need to know what Tony was up to?

Bear waited a minute, then crept toward the door and silently unlocked it. The moon was now behind the clouds and it was pitch-dark outside. Bear took several cautious steps out into the cool night.

Before his eyes had fully adjusted, the world exploded in flashes of brilliant light and excruciating pain as a heavy metal flashlight smashed into the back of his head. Bear crumbled to the ground.

CHAPTER 63

ROSE

ROSE STARTLED AWAKE, HER HEART beating fast. She must have dozed off. Where was Bear? She looked around the now dark room, wondering what had woken her. As Rose stared through the storeroom's small dusty window at the woods beyond, she thought she heard someone at the door. Then, slowly, slowly, she saw the doorknob turning. In a panic, she began running her hands over the sleeping bag, frantically trying to find her phone.

Crack! The door flew open, slamming into the wall, and a dark figure holding a large silver flashlight stepped into the room. As the light played around the room, Rose hunched in the corner, unable to breathe. As the beam came nearer, she bolted off the mattress, hoping against hope that she could make it to the door into the main room of the store where she could hide.

Tony grabbed wildly for her, catching nothing but air. He lunged forward, trying again as Rose stumbled toward the door. This time, he caught a handful of her long hair. Rose's head snapped back and she screamed. Tony dragged her back into the storeroom, her arms flailing and her heels banging against the floor. He threw her onto the mattress.

"I've been looking everywhere for you, bitch. You didn't think you could just disappear, did you?"

Rose pressed herself into the corner, hoping to feel her phone as she scooted across the mattress.

"You're coming back with me. You're my wife, God dammit, and we've gotta fix things."

"Tony, you know I can't go back," Rose whispered. Tony's hand shot out fast as a lizard's tongue and connected viciously with Rose's cheek, leaving a large red welt. Rose's hand went to her cheek. She bit her lip, determined not to cry. Somehow, she had to convince Tony that he had to let her go.

"Tony, you know I loved you and we tried, but it didn't work for us. It's too late now."

Tony stared at Rose incredulously. "You don't get it, do you, bitch? My job is gone. My house is gone. My friends are gone. Even my parents don't answer my calls. This is *your* fault. *You* did this to me. You have to come back and fix it." Tony's breathing was ragged now, his fists compulsively clenching and unclenching.

Rose started to shake her head. Tony edged closer, the flashlight beam now blinding her.

"Get up."

Rose dodged Tony's outstretched arm. "No, Tony!"

Tony's frustration and anger erupted. "Rose, I'm giving you one last chance to get up!"

"Tony, I can't." Rose began to sob.

"God damn it!" Tony took a full swing and smashed Rose's head with the flashlight. Rose spun around, the back of her head hitting the wall with a sickening thud. She slumped on the mattress. Blood was streaked down the wall and was now pooling beneath her head.

Tony stared at her coldly. This wasn't what he had been hoping for. But he was a realist. He had come prepared.

Tony walked out the door and knelt by Bear, trying to check for a pulse. He couldn't find one. Still, he didn't want to take any chances. He hooked his arms under Bear's and began dragging him, straining to slide the dead weight across the sparse grass. He had to get him inside by Rose. Halfway to the storeroom door, his chest heaving and his shoulders aching, he gave up. Bear was just too heavy, and he was running out of time. He dropped Bear's body on the grass and strode across the field behind the store to his partially hidden car. He popped the trunk and removed two heavy gas cans.

CHAPTER 64

BEAR

Slowly, sensations began to penetrate Bear's brain, dragging him back to consciousness. The skin on his arms and face was searingly hot, as though he were lying in a large oven. Intense pain coursed through his head, pulsing with each beat of his heart. Then he smelled it—the unmistakable scent of gasoline.

Bear groaned and tried to open his eyes. The nighttime sky above him was strangely orange. Gritting his teeth, he turned his head slightly. Oh my God, the back of the store was burning. Rose! Bear forced himself to sit up.

Head pounding, Bear worked his phone out of his back pocket and, acting on instinct, speed dialed his mom. "Ma! The store's on fire. Rose is inside. Call 911 right away. I'm going in!"

CHAPTER 65

ALICE

ALICE BOLTED UPRIGHT A SECOND time, fumbling for her phone. Bear again! Alice's dream–muddled brain cleared in an instant as she listened to Bear. "No, no!" she cried, but Bear had already hung up. Then she heard it, the wail of the town's fire alarm calling the volunteer firefighters to work.

Panic washed over Alice. What should she do? Call 911. Bear said to call 911. Hands shaking, Alice stared at the phone she was still holding in one hand. She dialed.

"911, what's your emergency?"

"The empty liquor store on the old highway—it's on fire!"

"Are you at the store, ma'am?"

"No."

"Do you have an address for the store?"

Address? Really? Didn't they know it? Then, out of nowhere, the words popped out of Alice's mouth: "5908 Layhill Road—on Route 2."

"We've already received a call about the fire, ma'am, and emergency personnel are on the way. Are you sure you're OK?"

"Yes, yes. But my son and his girlfriend are inside the store. You've got to tell the firefighters. And hurry!"

Alice staggered out of her chair, grabbed her keys and ran to her car.

CHAPTER 66

BEAR

BEAR PULLED HIMSELF TO HIS feet and lurched to the open storeroom door. Flames had already consumed the doorway and were now climbing the walls of the back of the store.

"Rose!" After pulling up his shirt, Bear threw himself through the doorway. He stumbled across the storeroom, his arm over his face, trying to ward off the heat from the flames. He began coughing uncontrollably, the super–heated smoke searing his lungs. Remembering a lesson he had learned on a childhood visit to the town firehouse, he dropped to his hands and knees and crawled toward the mattress in the corner of the room. Thank God. Rose.

Moving as quickly as he could, Bear crawled to her side and began pulling her limp body off the mattress. Bear looked behind him. The path to the back door was impassable as the fire spread up the walls and across the ceiling, dropping burning chunks of wood to the floor.

Bear pulled his shirt up over his face again and began dragging Rose as he staggered backwards toward the front of the store.

I'm so sorry, Rose. I'm so sorry, Rose. The words played over and over in his mind. He could hear sirens in the distance now. *Thank God.* But it was getting so hard. He couldn't breathe, and the fire was catching up to him. *Keep going. You've got to keep going.* He made it to the main part of the store, but couldn't see across the room through the smoke. Relying solely on memory, Bear kept pulling. *Hang on, Rose.*

A burning timber fell in front of Bear and he tripped. He reached back around and grabbed Rose's hands and, now on his hands and knees, continued in what he hoped was the direction of the door. As another fit of uncontrollable coughing hit him, a light shone into the room, its beam barely visible through the smoke.

CHAPTER 67

HELEN

HELEN SAT IN THE ROCKER on Kim's front porch, sipping a tall glass of scotch and trying her best to forget the past week. After tossing and turning in bed for hours, she had finally gotten up, pulled on some clothes, and come outside. It was a beautiful night, replete with stars, a warm breeze, and the salty scent of the ocean. The new leaves on the trees in the yard were rustling softly.

But Helen was oblivious. It had been a week since she and Alice had gotten home, and she was still caught up in all the emotions of their disastrous trip. And then finding Dan at Alice's—in his bathrobe, no less. It had felt like a double–punch to the gut. Here she was miserable and worrying about her relationship with Alice, while Alice had moved right along and invited Dan for a weekend fling. Her feelings about that were too complex to even try to unravel tonight.

Helen had put so much time and effort into the store. And into their trip. For what? Sure, they had run into problems, and Helen had made some innocent mistakes. But what had Alice done? Alice hadn't spoken to her since they had gotten back. And, really, ditching her at the airport? Helen took another sip of scotch.

Clearly, their partnership had been ill–fated from the beginning. They were so different—complete opposites, in fact. And yet Helen had wanted it to work.

Helen startled as the town's fire station siren blasted. Must be a fire somewhere, she thought offhandedly.

Her thoughts returned to her quandary. What had she conceivably hoped to get out of this venture, and why did she feel so terrible now that everything had fallen apart with Alice?

Wow, must be a good–sized fire, thought Helen, as the sound of two fire engines racing by intruded once again on her thoughts.

Just then, Kim burst out the front door, her nightgown pale in the moonlight. "Mom! Get up! You haven't been answering your phone, so they called me. Irene from down on Backlick Road. The store's on fire! Come on! We've gotta go!"

"What? The store? You mean *my* store? And how can you go? You're in your nightgown, for God's sake! And what about the kids?" Helen rose unsteadily out of her chair, pushing her feet into her shoes.

Kim ran back into the house, returning in less than a minute zipping up an old pair of jeans and pulling a sweatshirt over her head. "Come on! Get in the car!"

Helen stood frozen. She glanced down, noticing with surprise that her hands were shaking, spilling tiny splashes of scotch all over the porch. She put the glass down and looked helplessly at Kim. "What am I supposed to do?"

"Get in the damn car."

Kim roared out of the driveway, narrowly missing the trash cans she had put out just hours before. Helen was shocked by the intensity of Kim's reaction. Why, she hadn't even fastened her seatbelt! Kim was on the phone with Kevin, asking him—no, *telling* him—that he had to come over to the house right away and stay with the kids. Helen's heart began to race as she stared through the windshield at the glow in the distance.

As Kim swung into the lot across the street from the store, Helen could hardly believe the surreal scene. She forced herself to step out of the car and follow Kim as they worked their way to the front of the growing crowd. The entire block was cast in a red light as large flames shot out of the roof at the back of the store. The fire's blistering heat felt like a prickly warning against the bare skin of her arm.

Helen started to tear up as the reality of what she was seeing sank in. All their work—gone. At least three fire trucks had arrived, and firefighters were donning gear, manhandling giant hoses, and shouting directions. A police cordon held back the growing crowd of onlookers.

Helen was in a daze as her eyes swept through the mass of people, finally coming to rest on one small lone figure on her hands and knees in the grass across the street. Alice! Helen pushed her way through the crowd and ran across the road, yelling at anyone who tried to intercept her that this was her store and they better get out of the way.

As Helen knelt in the grass by Alice, she realized Alice was wracked by sobs. “Alice, are you OK?” She instinctively threw her arms around Alice, wrapping her in a tight embrace.

Alice could barely speak. In starts and fits, she told Helen that Bear had gone into the store looking for Rose. Now three firefighters had gone in after Bear, but no one had come back out. Alice collapsed into Helen, soaking Helen’s shirt with her tears. Helen began to cry, too, as she held Alice, rocking her gently. “Don’t give up, Alice. Bear’s a strong man and he must know what he’s doing.” Then, as an afterthought, “But why would Rose be in the store at this time of night?”

“She was going to sleep there tonight. To hide out from her creepy husband who battered her and came from Colorado and beat up Bear this afternoon.”

Helen was aghast. “Oh, Alice. I’m so sorry.” Helen squeezed Alice even tighter.

Bear and Rose in the store? Oh, please God, let them be OK. Helen thought about how excited Bear had been about the store and how hard he had worked. She could see and hear Bear now, smiling and wrapping his arms around Alice and her, telling them to stop sniping at each other. He had been the glue that held them together. Please don’t let things end like this.

Kim came up and knelt behind her mother, placing her arms around her waist and her head on her shoulder. “I heard about Bear, Mom,” she whispered. “Any word?” Helen shook her head. She could feel Kim’s shuddering breaths as she fought back tears. What would Bear say if he saw us now? thought Helen. "Women!" he would say, shaking his head, but she knew he would be secretly pleased.

A commotion broke out at the front of the store as three firefighters tumbled out the door, half carrying, half pulling Bear and Rose. As soon as they were clear, the firefighters collapsed on the grass and steadier arms grabbed Bear and Rose, heading toward the waiting ambulances. They were both unconscious, and oxygen masks were slapped on their faces. The men carrying the inert mass of Bear were struggling, while Rose seemed to float through the air between her saviors. She was placed on a stretcher, then pushed into one of the ambulances, its sterile white interior packed with equipment offering hope but also fear. Bear was pushed into a second ambulance.

"Alice! Get up! It's Bear—he's out!" Helen, with Kim's help, pulled Alice to her feet, and they all ran.

"Bear!" Alice cried. "I'm here!"

Helen and Kim hung back as Alice scrambled into the ambulance with Bear and took Bear's big hands in hers. As the doors swung shut, they could hear Bear struggling to regain consciousness. Helen heard him asking in a raspy voice as he tried to wrestle the oxygen mask off his face, "Is Rose OK?"

The ambulances tore off into the night, sirens blaring. Helen stood watching them depart, her hands hanging at her side, her heart heavy. She turned to look at the store, but it was essentially gone.

CHAPTER 68

KIM

As Kim pulled into the parking lot at Calverton Methodist Hospital, she had flashbacks of coming here to visit her grandmother in her last days. It had been awful. And now Bear and Rose. Kim had passed on religion a long time ago, but she found herself repeating a prayer under her breath: *Please God, let them be all right. Please God.* She glanced at her mother in the seat beside her. Tear tracks were visible down her slightly sooty face. Why, she looks old, thought Kim with a bit of a shock. She parked the car and turned to her mother. "Come on, Mom, let's go."

The bright glare of the hospital lights hurt their eyes as they walked into the emergency room and over to the information desk. A pleasant, but vaguely uninterested woman looked up. "Can I help you?"

Kim looked the woman in the eye. "We're family of Bear Kowalski, who was brought in from a fire a few minutes ago.

"My, my, that boy's gotta lot of family." The woman smiled. "Brenda," the woman yelled at a nurse's aide who was passing by, "can you take these ladies to the family waiting room?"

Feeling powerful pulls of both eagerness and reluctance, Kim and Helen followed Brenda down a long, antiseptic hallway of highly polished brown and white tiles. When Brenda opened a door and ushered them into a family waiting room, Kim was stunned to find the room already partially full.

"Ah, more family, I see," said Bill, rising from his chair.

Kim was surprised when Bill, Millie, and Jed rushed over to her mom and wrapped her in a group hug. She was even more surprised as she watched her mom hug them back. Timmy and Willow gave Helen small waves and thumbs–ups from the tiny couch against the wall where they sat holding hands. Helen seemed incredibly relieved to see everyone.

"How did you all get here so fast?" asked Kim, looking around.

"We came straight from home as soon as we heard what was happening," answered Bill.

"And where's Alice?"

"They just took her back to get an update from the doctor. We're all waiting to hear."

Arranging chairs for her mom and herself, Kim sat down and faced the group. "So, what do we know?"

"Not much," said Millie. "This will be the first report on their condition."

"But how did this happen?" asked Kim. "Do we know how the fire started?" Everyone shook their heads. "Or what Rose and Bear were doing at the store at night?"

Millie looked at Kim. "Yeah—hiding out from Rose's soon–to–be ex–husband." Kim was shocked. "Rose was in a terribly abusive relationship with a guy named Tony while she lived in Denver. I first met her in a women's shelter in Boston after she drove all the way from Colorado to get away from Tony. At the time, he was in prison for assaulting her. Rose had heard he was out some time ago, and today, somehow, he found her. He showed up this afternoon at the café and then went to Bear's trailer looking for her. He punched and threatened Bear when he couldn't find her." Millie unconsciously wiped her eyes on her sleeve.

"But why would Rose be at Bear's trailer?" asked Kim.

Everyone in the group looked up. Helen answered. "Kim, Rose has been living with Bear for several months now."

Kim blinked. She should have seen that one coming.

CHAPTER 69

ALICE

At that moment, Alice pushed through the door, relief painted on her tear-streaked face. She paused, looking around the room.

"Oh, thank you all so much for being here. I think Bear's going to be fine. They've had to intubate him because of the swelling from the smoke inhalation so he's sedated now, but they're hoping they'll be able to switch him over to regular oxygen in a couple of days. And he's got a nasty concussion."

Everyone rushed to give Alice a hug. Alice melted into the embrace, but then abruptly pulled back.

"But the news about Rose isn't as good. They're helicoptering her to a hospital in Boston where she can get more advanced treatment. She was exposed to the smoke longer than Bear, and the damage is more extensive. Plus, she got a lot of stitches in her head and they're monitoring her closely for brain injury. Fortunately, they both have only minor burns." Bill pulled a chair over toward Alice and she collapsed into it gratefully.

Millie pulled her jacket on. "Listen, guys, I'm going to Boston. I've got to be with Rose." Millie started to tear up. "She's like a sister to me."

"Do you know if she has any family?" Kim asked.

"No. Both her parents are dead and she doesn't have any brothers or sisters."

"What about the café?" asked Bill.

"Well, it will just have to close for a few days. I'll call Ann and she can notify the staff and put a sign in the window."

"Let me walk you out, Millie," said Bill. "And don't you worry. We're not going to leave you stranded in Boston. We've got enough good people in this town that we can take care of both Bear and Rose. Alice, we'll check back tomorrow."

As Millie and Bill headed out the door, Jed stood up, too. "I better get back to the farm and fill Chrissie in. And I second what Bill said, Alice. We all would do anything for Bear and Rose—and you. We'll make this work." He gave Alice a squeeze and followed the others out the door with Timmy and Willow close behind.

Alice slumped back into her chair, both emotionally and physically drained. Helen was the first to speak.

"Alice, I'm truly sorry. For everything." She grabbed Alice's hand.

"Me, too, Helen. We sure are two stubborn old mules!"

"You know I'll do anything to help. Do you want to go home and get some rest and I'll stay here?"

Alice shook her head. "Thanks, Helen, but I think I'll stay a little longer just to make sure everything's all right. Then I'll head home. There's really nothing to do while he's sedated. The doctor said I should be sure and get some rest before they take the tube out and he wakes up."

"OK. But you'll call—right? Anytime. Anything you need."

"I will. Thank you, Helen."

Alice and Helen stood and embraced.

Kim put her arms around the two older women.

CHAPTER 70

ALICE

ALICE WATCHED AS HELEN AND Kim walked back down the sterile hallway, through the big doors, and out into the elevator lobby. She began the slow trudge back to Bear's room, the weight of her physical and emotional exhaustion so heavy she could barely lift her feet. As she neared the corner, she heard a frantic knocking on the thick glass window of the doors to the elevator lobby. Slightly annoyed, she stopped and turned, wondering who could possibly be here at this hour.

Good grief, it was Dan! Alice hurried back down the hallway, hit the Open button and exclaimed, "Dan! What are you doing here?"

"Well, I got a somewhat hysterical call from Helen a few hours ago—this is starting to become a regular thing with you ladies—so I got back in the car and drove straight to the hospital. Sounded like you might need some help. I hope that's OK."

"OK? It's great." Alice's eyes filled with tears. "I can't believe you would come all this way."

"That's what good friends do, Alice. Besides, it's not that far. How are Bear and Rose?"

"They're doin' well, especially Bear. They've had to transfer Rose by helicopter to a hospital in Boston."

Alice and Dan walked to Bear's room. Alice talked the whole time, filling Dan in on Bear's and Rose's conditions. Alice pushed the heavy door open and they entered the hospital room with its soft beeps and whooshes of air. They both stopped and looked at Bear.

"Don't worry, Dan, Bear's out for the night. They told me I should go on home, but I just don't want to leave him. I came so close to losing him tonight." Alice ran her hands down the sheet next to Bear smoothing invisible wrinkles, as tears slid down her cheeks. She trusted the nurses and doctors implicitly, but, still, seeing Bear with all the tubes and the breathing machine was enough to undo her.

"Knowing you even as little as I do, Alice, that's just what I figured. Then it occurred to me that you seemed to find me a quite satisfactory pillow, so here I am. Let's sit down and see if we can get you comfortable so you can get some rest. I'm afraid I'll have to leave around 5:30 to get back to Boston for a court appearance at 9, but until then, I'm all yours."

"I told everybody to leave, but I didn't really want to be alone. How can I ever thank you?"

"Just leave me a little room."

Alice and Dan settled on the small couch next to Bear's bed. Alice talked for a while, telling Dan everything she knew about Tony. She was determined to stay awake and never take her eyes off of Bear and his rhythmic breathing. Within a half hour, she was asleep. Nurses came and went, monitors beeped, distant alarms rang in the hallway, but Alice barely stirred. When she finally woke around 6, Dan was gone. A hand-written note lay on the foot of Bear's bed: *Great night again, Alice!* Alice smiled as she snatched it up and stuffed it in her pocket.

CHAPTER 71

ALICE

Late the next morning Alice was getting herself a cup of coffee in the family waiting room when Bill and Helen arrived. She put down her half-full cup and crossed the room to give them each a quick hug.

"Did you get any rest, Alice?" asked Helen, giving Alice a quick once–over. She looked surprisingly refreshed.

"Not too bad actually. Dan was here." Alice could tell from the look on Helen's face that Helen thought she was imagining things. "I wasn't dreaming this, Helen. He said you called him last night and that you sounded kind of hysterical. According to Dan, he's getting rather used to midnight calls for help from the two of us!"

"Well, yes, I did call him. For some reason I thought I should let him know. I hope that was OK."

"It was great, Helen. He was able to stay until around 5:30, and I was actually able to get some sleep."

"So what's the latest on Bear and Rose?" asked Bill, still trying to figure out who this Dan guy was.

"I saw the doctor this morning, and he says that Bear's swelling and breathing are already improving. He's still got the tube in, but his color's a lot better. I'm so relieved."

"That's great news," said Helen. "Any update on Rose?"

"I spoke to Millie a little while ago. They've moved Rose into something called a hyperbaric chamber to make her breathing easier, and that seems to help a lot. Millie sounded optimistic, but I got the sense her recovery is going to take a lot longer."

"Still, that's all wonderful news, given the circumstances," said Bill. "It sounds like it was a good end to a terrible night. Meanwhile, Helen and I have been busy. By early this morning, everybody in town had heard about the fire and wanted to know how they could help. So, Helen set up a spreadsheet, and people are volunteering to spell Millie in Boston. That way Millie doesn't have to stay there all the time and Rose is never alone. And Helen is insistent that she is staying here to help you."

Helen smiled. "I am at your command, Alice. You better take advantage of this once–in–a–lifetime opportunity!"

"And you don't need to worry about food. Meals are being delivered to your next–door neighbor, Mrs. Porter, and she's agreed to keep everything and bring whatever you need whenever you need it."

Alice closed her eyes. "I am so grateful. I don't know what I would do without my friends."

Just then a knock came at the door. Bill stepped around Alice and let Patrick Graves into the room.

Looking terribly awkward with his sheriff's hat in his hand, Patrick took a step toward Alice. "Alice, I hate to intrude. But I've got some questions for you. Helen, it's good you're here, too."

Bill looked inquiringly at Helen and Alice. "Bill, do you mind staying?" asked Alice softly.

They all took seats, wondering what Patrick had going to say.

"Well, first, I'm awfully sorry about the fire, and Claire and I are praying for a swift recovery for Bear and Rose."

"Thank you, Patrick."

"As soon as we got the fire out last night, our investigation started. We've called in the investigators from the fire department in Calverton since they have a lot more experience with arson."

"Arson!" Alice, Helen and Bill all looked horrified. The thought had crossed each of their minds, but still … hearing it confirmed was something else entirely.

"I'm afraid so. It looks like an accelerant, most likely gasoline, was poured around the back of the building and then lit." Patrick shifted uncomfortably in his seat and stared at the floor. “Bear came by yesterday and told me about Rose Marchetti’s husband, Tony Walsh. He certainly seems like the most likely suspect. We know he’s driving a black sports car with Colorado tags, but my guess is he’s already miles away from here. Is there anything you can tell me about him that might help us find him?”

Alice, Helen, and Bill shook their heads. “You should ask Millie,” said Alice. “Millie can give you a physical description. And you might find him in the Denver police records. Millie said something about a restraining order having been issued there and an assault conviction.”

“Thanks, Alice.” Patrick rose to leave. “I’ll keep you posted, and you let me know as soon as we can talk to Bear or Rose. And watch your step.” Patrick nervously tipped his hat and walked rather hurriedly out the door.

Alice, Helen, and Bill exchanged quizzical looks. “Anyone else think there was something a little odd about that conversation?” asked Alice.

CHAPTER 72

ALICE

ALICE WAS DOZING IN THE chair by Bear's bed later that afternoon when a nurse gently touched her arm. "Alice," she whispered. Alice jerked awake.

"Is Bear OK?"

"Yes. Sorry to wake you, but there's someone out by the elevator, wanting to talk to you."

Alice pushed herself out of the chair, decided not to look in the mirror, and quietly let herself out of the room. When she got to the big doors leading out to the lobby, she could see Brendan Larson waiting.

Oh, great. Come to tell me I have to pay for my sins or something.

Alice considered turning back before he saw her. Just the sight of him made her face burn as she thought of him telling her to leave Faye's funeral. But no—why should she let him intimidate her? She wasn't going to skulk around Poplar Point hoping she wouldn't run into him.

Alice hit the big Open Door button and walked out. "Hello, Brendan. You wanted to see me?"

Brendan looked utterly dejected. The old swagger and booming voice seemed to have abandoned him.

"Is there somewhere we can talk?"

Reminding herself of her old goal of compassion, Alice led Brendan to the now–familiar family waiting room where they both took seats.

After wringing his hands for a moment, Brendan looked up. "I heard about Bear, Alice. I'm so sorry. I'm sure you don't want to talk to me right now, but I had to come apologize to you and to ask for your forgiveness."

Alice sat up a little straighter.

"I was wrong to have been rude to you at Faye's funeral. I know that now. I was just so upset and so angry. I blamed myself for Faye's death, for having left her alone so much. When you walked up—well, I just directed all my anger at you. And now this has happened to Bear. I never wanted any of this to happen. I needed you to know this."

Alice looked at Brendan a little more closely. He seemed sincere.

"I appreciate the apology, Brendan. But Bear's going to be OK, and you mustn't blame yourself for Faye's death."

Brendan looked back down at his hands. His voice shook. "You don't understand, Alice. Faye didn't die of a heart attack like I told everyone. She killed herself." Alice sat back, her mouth hanging open. "She'd been depressed for years and she was drinking and taking pills. We'd been to all sorts of doctors and therapists. Then it started getting worse this past year. But I was tired of it all—and busy. I thought my life had taken on a larger purpose—that I had been called to save Poplar Point."

Alice looked down, shaking her head. "I'm so sorry, Brendan."

Brendan seemed terribly distraught. Alice impulsively reached out and took his hands in hers. "Brendan, I talked to Faye around the time of the Town Meeting and she was not herself. She was clearly distressed, and the pain must have just become more than she could bear."

Brendan's hands trembled. "I knew everything was getting worse, but I thought I could wait, that I had more time to deal with it."

"I can't imagine how you must feel. I'm sure you'll need some time to work through your grief and regret." Brendan looked up, his eyes shining with tears. "You know, Brendan, I haven't been to church for quite a few years. But I do remember what you said. You can give in to all the anger and guilt and anguish. Or you can remember Faye as she was before all her problems held her in their grip. Then forgive yourself as you have so often preached and make the most of the time you have left."

Alice couldn't believe she was sitting here giving spiritual advice to the town minister. Maybe this is what all those hours of meditation, study, and reflection had been leading her to.

"And don't worry about me, Brendan. We've known each other forever, and we're both very passionate people who can sometimes get carried away. Let me know if I can help."

Alice and Brendan stood up, still grasping each other's hands.

"I have to go to Bear now."

"Of course. Thank you, Alice, for being so understanding."

Alice watched Brendan walk down the hall and through the double doors. He seemed much smaller than she remembered.

CHAPTER 73

HELEN

THE NEXT MORNING, HELEN KNOCKED with her elbow on the door to Bear's room and, after hearing Alice's "Come in," pushed through the door carrying a large vase filled with bright spring flowers. Alice was sitting in her usual chair by Bear's bed, her hand on his arm. She seemed a lot calmer.

Helen put the vase on the shelf by the window and pulled a chair up next to Alice. "How's he doing?" Then she looked more closely. "The tube's gone!"

"Yup. The nurse took it out early this morning and now we're just waiting for the sedation to wear off."

Helen grabbed Alice's hand. "That's great! Progress at last!"

The two women sat side by side staring at Bear, willing him to wake. After a few moments, they began to talk quietly. Helen couldn't believe Alice's story about Brendan—poor man. Although he had been a real jerk at times. And Alice was reduced to tears by Helen's recounting of everything the town was doing, particularly the money they had raised.

The past 24 hours had passed in a blur for Helen. She had worked hard, serving as the coordinator and point of contact for all the help that had poured in from the town. Helen was amazed at how everyone was pitching in, even signing up to drive to Boston to spend hours sitting by Rose, someone most of them barely knew. Bill had set up a donation station at the hardware store and had collected enough money to cover the cost of a motel room by the hospital in Boston. For the first time in years, maybe ever, Helen felt a part of the town. At last, their conversation turned to the store.

"Have you been by the store, Helen?"

"I have. It's a disaster."

Alice held her head in her hands. "After all our work. What a waste." Helen placed her hand on Alice's knee. When Alice looked up, she was surprised to see Helen grinning.

"Well, I've got some good news for you, Alice. Been waiting for the right moment to tell you. I never mentioned it last fall, because I knew how tight you and Bear were getting with money. I was pretty sure you wouldn't approve, but I got us a great big insurance policy anyway. I had Matt check and we're sure—arson is covered so long as it's not arson by owner. That should be pretty easy for us to prove." Helen was beaming, clearly feeling very proud of herself.

Alice smiled, then burst out laughing. "Well, I'll be. If that don't beat them all, Helen! I swear I will never question your judgment again!"

"Don't get carried away, Alice."

"You're right." Alice's eyes sparkled. "There's still that problem of a little jail time I seem to remember." Alice pointed and shook her finger at Helen, but Helen couldn't wipe the grin off her face.

Helen reached into her bag, extracting a neatly typed piece of paper. "We need some documentation to get the insurance claim filed. Here's a list of the papers I need you to find."

"Yes, ma'am!" Bear, woken by the noise, opened one eye and was surprised to see his mom saluting Helen while they both laughed. He drifted back to sleep.

CHAPTER 74

BEAR

"Alice! Bear just opened his eyes!"

Bear stared at Alice and Helen uncomprehendingly. Where was he? Why was he here? He groaned, and croaked, "Water."

Alice and Helen lunged for the water pitcher, but Helen pulled back just in time. Bear took a tiny sip from a straw and closed his eyes again. He felt his mom gently wrap her arms around his neck and rest her head softly on his forehead. "Everything's OK, Bear," she whispered.

Moments later, Bear's eyes fluttered open again. "Rose. Where's Rose, Ma?"

"She's doin' fine, honey. Don't you worry. You saved her!"

As the memory of the fire began to return, Bear grew more and more agitated. "I heard his car," Bear whispered.

"Whose car?"

"That bastard, Tony. His car's got a bad muffler, and I heard it. I opened the door, Ma, and he hit me. I couldn't get her, Mom." Bear started to cry, which triggered yet another painful coughing spell.

"But you did get her, Bear. She's going to be fine." Alice turned her head. "Helen, can you call Patrick? He's gotta hear this."

Patrick was there in minutes, the strain of the investigation showing in the new lines around his eyes.

"Bear, how are you feelin'?"

Bear stared at Patrick for a minute. He couldn't quite remember why, but he found something about Patrick deeply unsettling. Bear haltingly told Patrick the little he remembered.

Bear's arms and legs were trembling under the warm blanket as he recounted all he remembered. What if he hadn't come to? What if he hadn't found Rose? Bear forced himself to focus. "Where's Tony?"

"We've sent out an all–points bulletin asking everyone to be on the lookout for him or his car. But we're assuming he's headed back to Colorado since no one's seen him around here since the fire."

"Is someone with Rose?" Bear couldn't shake the feeling of dread that had wrapped itself around him.

Alice patted Bear on the leg. "Now don't you worry about anything. Rose is in a hospital in Boston, and Millie is with her. She's going to be fine."

Patrick gave Bear his best look of reassurance. "We haven't publicized her location at all, Bear. She's safe. I'll let you all know the minute we hear anything about Tony."

Bear could feel the tension in his body let go a bit. But he wasn't going to relax until he had talked to Rose. Until he had seen her. Maybe he could get out of the hospital tomorrow and have his mom drive him to Boston. If only he could keep his eyes open....

CHAPTER 75

ALICE

A WEEK HAD PASSED, AND Alice's knees were killing her. Dust swirled around her head and tickled her nose as she moved boxes. What the hell was she doing up here in the attic?

Brushing a stray gray hair out of her face, Alice settled back uncomfortably on the cushion she had carried up with her and was surprised to find a tear lazily snaking its way down one cheek.

She was so grateful that Bear was out of the hospital and that Rose was doing better. Not surprisingly, Bear had moved up to Boston to be with Rose. Still, what a disaster. For months, she and Helen and Bear had weathered their ups and downs, keeping their noses to the grindstone as they pursued this crazy idea of a cannabis store in Poplar Point. And now here they were—practically back at square one, with a burned–out store and Bear and Rose's attacker still on the run.

Alice rubbed her aching knees as she looked around, overwhelmed by the piles of boxes, old furniture, books, clothes, and photo albums, much of it dating back to her mother's youth. A wave of sadness swept over her as she thought about how much she missed her mother and Arlo, and how close she had come to losing Bear. Alice resignedly turned her attention back to her search for the store files. Alice wasn't sure why Helen insisted she needed them now, but Helen usually had a good reason, even if her requests sometimes came across more like orders.

Aha! Progress! A box with the store's address on it. But then the box next to it caught her eye. A box with her mother's name on it, written in the perfect looping script so assiduously practiced by girls of her time. Alice couldn't resist.

Alice pried the lid off and there was her mother, standing under the elm tree in the side yard, a flowered sundress fluttering around her knees, her dark hair falling across her shoulders, her feet in white platform sandals. She was so pretty! Alice sifted through the box's contents—more pictures of her mother, her grandparents, even herself as a baby and then a toddler proudly taking her first steps. Everyone was beaming. Could life really have been so simple once? Or was it that simple? Alice continued searching through the pictures, looking for a picture of the father she had never seen. According to her mother, he had died in an accident before she was born. And that was the end of the story. A mysterious tale of tragedy that was never embellished upon, never discussed.

Beneath the jumble of pictures, Alice found a single envelope with the words RUTHIE / PRIVATE printed all in caps across the front. Alice didn't recognize the handwriting. What was this? Letters in her family were a rarity since most everyone stayed in Poplar Point.

Alice's nerves tingled and a small wave of guilt washed over her as she slid her fingernail beneath the envelope's dried-out flap, carefully prying the thin paper apart. She gingerly extracted and then opened a letter, spreading it out on her lap. She began to read.

December 19, 1966

Darling Ruthie,

You said I must never contact you again, but I feel like I am losing my mind. I saw you on Main Street last week walking into the Friendly's Market with Alice's little hand in yours, and all I wanted to do was jump out of the car and run to you both. I know in my head that our time together was a sin, one that I must pay for every day of my life. And I know that, for everyone's sake, we must keep it a secret. But in my heart I want to sweep you and our daughter up in my arms, declaring my love for all the world to see.

I am terribly sorry for Margaret, having to live with a man who she knows loves another. But living day after day with her wrath is truly hell.

Margaret's eyes are filled with nothing but contempt when she looks at me, and I suspect she does not treat you much better when she thinks no one else is looking. The only thing that keeps us together is Helen. Thank God for Helen. She is the only joy in my life.

I will do my best not to write again, but I need you to know that you and Alice are never out of my mind. I will love you forever.

Henry

Alice sat back on her cushion, her hands trembling slightly, her mouth half open. Her mind was racing, trying to make sense of what she had just read. What was this? What did it mean? Was it true?

Alice unsteadily pushed herself off the cushion and half–walked, half crawled to the attic ladder. Clinging tightly to the handrail on one side, she side–stepped her way down to the hallway floor and then down the stairs to the kitchen door, thinking all the while. Yes, it looked like Mrs. Porter was sitting as usual in her porch swing next door.

Gathering her courage, Alice pushed through the door and walked purposefully across the lawn, letter in hand.

"Alice, dear. How lovely to see you! Please, come have a seat. Would you like a glass of lemonade?"

Alice, usually so polite and rarely lacking for conversation, wordlessly handed the letter to Mrs. Porter. A quizzical look on her face, Mrs. Porter fumbled in the side pocket of her faded house dress for her glasses and then began to read. When she finished, she stared at her gnarled hands for a minute before reluctantly raising her eyes to meet Alice's.

"Is this true? Was Henry Newbold ... my father?"

Mrs. Porter coughed. "Yes," she said quietly.

"And no one ever told me? Who knows? Does the whole town know? Does Helen know? Why didn't anyone ever tell me?"

"No, honey, of course Helen doesn't know. A few of the old folks in town figured it out, but your mother and grandmother asked us all never to speak of it. You know how hard it is to keep a secret in a small town like Poplar Point, but we all agreed that it was best for everyone, particularly you and Helen, if we let your mother stick to her story and let bygones be bygones. Of course, Margaret was unable to let things go, and it was hard to watch her dislike for your mother fester over the years. Margaret, in particular, never forgave Henry. The only person she ever truly loved again was Kim. But Margaret was no more anxious than your mother to have the truth come out."

Alice was speechless. She stared at Mrs. Porter for a moment, then walked back across the yard, her heart beating fast, her fists clenched by her sides. How could her mother have never told her? And what kind of man was her father to have created this mess? How might her life have been different if she had known that she had a father who loved her? It was hard to even begin to unravel all the damage that had been done as a result of this one fateful decision. But then what would have happened if she and Helen had known, if the whole town had known? I have to tell Helen—and Bear and Kim. How can this be??

CHAPTER 76

ALICE

Later that evening, Alice sat in her usual chair, hands twisting restlessly in her lap. Helen and Kim sat uncomfortably side by side on the couch, and Bear, who had driven down from Boston, perched on the edge of a hard wooden chair brought in from the dining room. They all stared at Alice curiously, wondering what could have possibly possessed her to call them and insist that they come over tonight. Was she pulling out of the store?

"I'm sure you're wondering why I've called you all here." Alice fought back tears. Her voice quivering, she went on, "Earlier today I was up in the attic looking through some old boxes. I found something—a letter—a very upsetting letter. I felt you all had a right to see it, too." Alice handed the letter to Helen. "Helen, maybe you can read this out loud so that Bear and Kim can hear it, too."

Helen looked at Alice, a hint of trepidation in her eyes. As Helen read, Alice could see an array of emotions play across her face, much as they must have played across her own earlier in the day. Confusion, shock, anger, beginning understanding.

When she finished, Helen locked eyes with Alice. "Did you know about this?"

"No, of course not."

"Do you think it's true?"

"It seems like it. I went over to Mrs. Porter's today and she confirmed it. In fact, she said a few people in the town knew the entire story, but everyone kept quiet because they assumed it would be better for us."

"So, let me get this straight," interjected Bear. "The two of you are half–sisters?"

"It looks that way," Alice replied, her eyes never leaving Helen's.

Kim raised an eyebrow as she caught Bear's eye. "Wow," Bear mouthed to her silently. A tiny smile twitched at the corner of each of their mouths as they thanked the powers that be for the ultimately amicable end to their oh–so–brief romantic encounter.

Helen sighed. "Alice, I don't know what to say. I've thought a lot about why our mothers never got along. I guess I figured they were just very different from each other. But I never expected something like this. If it's true, it explains a lot."

"I'm damned flabbergasted myself. And I do think it's true. Maybe I'm imagining things now as I'm trying to make sense of this, but I remember how your dad always smiled at my mother and me but never came near us. And his hair was always thick and a little outta control like mine. I mean, it's kind of amazing. To think that all those years I actually had a dad, and he lived right here. I can't figure out whether I'm happy, sad, or super pissed."

"I think it's terribly sad," Kim said quietly, looking hesitantly at her mother out of the corner of her eye. "A true–life love triangle that broke everyone's hearts with all sorts of unseen consequences for two little girls. Mom growing up with parents in an unhappy marriage, and Alice never knowing her father. Each of you an only child not knowing you had a half–sister just down the street."

"Well," said Bear, "I think it's amazing. I'm glad you finally learned the truth."

Helen and Alice stared at each other, the cracks widening in a long–standing wall conceived before their births, built without their knowledge, and grounded in both love and hate.

PART 3

Six Months Later

CHAPTER 77

BEAR

BEAR STOOD IN THE PARKING lot at the Safe Access Dispensary greeting newcomers and directing folks to parking spaces, his spirits soaring. There was nothing like a fall day in New England. Puffy white clouds were scattered across the deep blue sky, and leaves, their brilliant oranges, reds and yellows only a distant memory, covered the ground.

Business at the store had settled into a steady stream of customers, both old and new, and the store had already surpassed its revenue expectations. Everyone was feeling super excited. Even the townspeople who had predicted disaster seemed impressed by the professionalism of the operation.

The first few weeks had been overwhelming with tons of people from all over stopping by to check out the new store. Bear was incredibly relieved that he was no longer having to shuttle customers back and forth from an over–flow parking lot.

Just as he was ready to walk back into the store, an old black Mercedes convertible pulled into the parking lot, crunching the gravel as it whipped into a prime parking spot. Matt! Bear rushed over, hand outstretched.

"Hey, man! Checkin' up on us?" Bear's usual wide grin lit up his face.

"Nah. Just too nice a day to sit behind a desk."

"You got that right. Come on in. We're pretty busy today, as you can see, but I'm sure I can rustle you up a cup of coffee."

Matt pocketed his keys, and the two men walked into the newest Safe Access Dispensary. Bear loved the aura of the place, and he could tell Matt liked it, too. Although he hoped never to have to live through another experience like the fire and all the ensuing pain, he thought again about how the destruction of the old building had been a blessing in disguise—thanks to Helen, of course. Everything was new, carefully considered, and thoroughly negotiated by Helen and his mom. Alice had achieved the homey feel she had wanted, with burnished pine flooring, old wood display cases, and a large wood stove. And Helen had her sleek, modern, but comfortable stools for customers to sit on while discussing product. Per Matt's instructions, all the employees wore jeans and polos and were connected by headphones, enabling them to communicate and move efficiently among the customers, providing prompt personal service. Helen had initially been horrified at the prospect of wearing jeans to work, but she seemed to have grown quite comfortable in her neatly–pressed, dry–cleaned designer jeans.

Bear and Matt spotted Rose talking animatedly with a customer. Rose looked fantastic, considering the weeks she had spent in the hospital. The pain had been horrific, but Rose had been a trooper, fighting her way to a full recovery. Once he had been discharged from the hospital, Bear had never left Rose's side.

"So, how's married life treating you, Bear?"

"No complaints so far!" No one had been too surprised that Bear and Rose had gotten married at the Town Hall as soon as they heard Rose's divorce had come through.

"And what's the latest with that asshole, Tony?"

"Still in prison, still awaiting trial. Rose and I don't look forward to having to relive everything when the trial finally rolls around, but we've been assured that Tony won't be seeing the light of day for quite some time. The strangest thing is that Tony's parents have reached out to Rose, trying to make amends. They've even offered to pay for Rose's hospital bills. We've talked about it a lot with Ma and Helen, and we all agree that Rose needs to make a clean break from that family. Of course, Rose is Rose, and she's tried to be as kind about it as she can."

"Well, I'm just glad you don't have to be looking over your shoulder all the time for Tony."

As Bear and Matt continued their walk around the store, Bear introduced Matt to the four new bud tenders, each of whom had gone through the rigorous training program Matt had designed. Matt really had the business down to a science, and Bear was once again grateful to Helen for having pushed them to work with him.

"Speaking of your mom and Helen, are they here, Bear?" Matt started walking toward the offices in the back.

"They're not here right now."

Matt stopped. "Oh? Where are they? I was hoping to spend a little time with them."

"Honestly, Matt, I don't know. They claim the 13th of every month is their anniversary—the anniversary of the night Ma found Helen drunk on the sidewalk in front of Sharky's."

Matt raised an eyebrow.

Bear waved his arm toward the front of the store. "In some ways, that's when all this began. So, the 13th of every month, whatever day of the week it is, they take a couple of hours off and meet somewhere to talk. They alternate picking the spot to meet—you know how competitive they can be."

Matt nodded knowingly.

"So today is the 13th and they're off somewhere talking, but I have no idea where. They should be back shortly."

Matt inhaled deeply and smiled. "Anything to foster good relations."

"Yeah, I know, Matt. We would all love to be a fly on the wall with the two of them. I wouldn't say they have exactly turned into devoted sisters, but they clearly care about each other and are working hard to make up for lost time.

Matt nodded and looked at Bear. "Honestly, Bear, I never would have imagined…."

CHAPTER 78

ALICE

ALICE PULLED HER SUBARU INTO a tight parking spot by the town square and got out of the car, feeling just the teensiest bit annoyed with Helen. She was always a bit apprehensive about Helen's choices of meeting places.

"Alice! Alice! I'm over here!"

Alice looked across the square at Helen sitting on a bucket swing in the town's playground, her trim ankles neatly crossed in front of her, her right arm waving in the air. Oh, great, thought Alice. Children's swings.

Alice marched toward the swings disgruntledly. "Helen, you don't actually expect me to fit into one of these swings, do you?"

Helen seemed momentarily taken aback. She looked at Alice. She looked at the swings. "Well, yes. I'm sure you can do this, Alice."

Alice walked over to a nearby picnic table and placed her bags on it, then approached the swing next to Helen's. If Helen could do this, then she guessed she could, too.

Alice sat on the swing, wedging her hips in as best she could. Alice looked up at the chains holding the broad strip of the swing between them. Something was going to have to give!

"Come on, Alice! Pump! See if you can touch the tree branch with your feet!"

Helen was smiling.

Alice started pumping. In defiance of gravity, her swing slowly rose in the air next to Helen's.

"Come on, Alice! We can do it!"

Alice pumped harder, her smaller arc gradually approaching Helen's. Suddenly, Alice saw her. A girl in a neatly pressed red plaid dress, knee socks, and whitened saddles shoes. Helen.

Alice looked at Helen. Their eyes connected as they swung up, hitched momentarily in the air, then fell back.

"This is so much fun!" yelled Helen, delightedly.

Alice shouted back, "Yes!"

An elderly couple walking by on the sidewalk stopped to look at the two older women swinging. They shook their heads and moved along.

They both slowed, dragging their feet in the dirt. After coming to a complete stop, Alice gripped both chains and hoisted herself awkwardly out of the swing. Helen had already performed a neat little jump and was striding over to the nearby picnic table where a brown paper bag awaited them. Alice made her way to the table and sank onto the bench. As she gingerly lifted two hot coffees out of the bag, she raised her eyes to meet Helen's. "Helen, do you remember?"

Helen smiled. "Yes, I do. It was so much fun."

"I'd forgotten until we were swinging. It sure was a long time ago. But look where we are today. Who could have ever predicted that?"

"No one," agreed Helen.

Lightning Source UK Ltd.
Milton Keynes UK
UKHW010730010822
406672UK00002B/396